ONE MAN TOO MANY

Skye Fargo didn't like the odds facing him in
the Oro City saloon. A half-breed with a
throwing knife. A gunman with Colt .45 slung
low on both hips. And a mountain man with
hands more deadly than any knife or gun.

So Skye started cutting them down. The half-
breed went down with a slug between the
eyes when his knife buried itself in the bar a
couple of inches from Fargo's midriff. The
gunman went down with a gun in each hand
and his blood spraying over the sawdusted
floor.

Now only the mountain man was left. Trouble
was, the Trailsman had run out of bullets . . .

. . . and his chances of coming out alive went
from zero to none . . .

THE TRAILSMAN 75

COLORADO ROBBER

by

Jon Sharpe

A SIGNET BOOK

NEW AMERICAN LIBRARY

PUBLISHER'S NOTE

This book is a work of fiction. Names, characters, places, and incidents either are the product of the author's imagination or are used fictitiously, and any resemblance to actual persons, living or dead, events, or locales is entirely coincidental.

The first chapter of this book previously appeared in *White Hell*, the seventy-fourth volume in this series.

SIGNET TRADEMARK REG. U.S. PAT. OFF. AND FOREIGN COUNTRIES
REGISTERED TRADEMARK—MARCA REGISTRADA
HECHO EN CHICAGO. U.S.A.

SIGNET, SIGNET CLASSIC, MENTOR, ONYX, PLUME, MERIDIAN
and NAL BOOKS are published by NAL PENGUIN INC.,
1633 Broadway, New York, New York 10019

First Printing, March, 1988

1 2 3 4 5 6 7 8 9

PRINTED IN THE UNITED STATES OF AMERICA

The Trailsman

Beginnings . . . they bend the tree and they mark the man. Skye Fargo was born when he was eighteen. Terror was his midwife, vengeance his first cry. Killing spawned Skye Fargo, ruthless, cold-blooded murder. Out of the acrid smoke of gunpowder still hanging in the air, he rose, cried out a promise never forgotten.

The Trailsman they began to call him all across the West: searcher, scout, hunter, the man who could see where others only looked, his skills for hire but not his soul, the man who lived each day to the fullest, yet trailed each tomorrow. Skye Fargo, the Trailsman, the seeker who could take the wildness of a land and the wanting of a woman and make them his own.

October 1861—in the highest and roughest mining camps of Colorado Territory, where winter threatens to arrive at any moment, and greed and suspicion are a way of life . . . and death

1

Slate-gray clouds swirled ever lower, obliterating the summits of the soaring mountains. What remained below was a dismal view of one of the many mining camps in Colorado Territory.

They called it Buckskin Joe, after a swaggering mountain man who had discovered gold a year ago. Its raw, ramshackle buildings pressed along one edge of Buckskin Creek. Behind the single street rose a steep, barren, rock-strewn slope.

Not all that long ago, it had been pristinely beautiful. Now it was riddled with fresh stumps and strewn with logging slash. The ground was pockmarked with prospect holes and scarred by the waste dumps of several mines. The precipitous slope rose several hundred feet before mercifully vanishing into the swirling dark fog.

For the past six October days those clouds had been blocking the accustomed warmth of the sun. Even worse, they had formed an inexhaustible supply of drizzle. The stuff was too cold to be rain but too fluid to be snow. This wretched weather overpowered slickers and buffalo robes. It slithered beneath clothes and crawled into a man's sinews and bones. It made his muscles stiff, brittle, uncooperative.

So Skye Fargo was just as glad that, for a change, he wasn't out in it this morning. Five days of such misery outdoors, heading south for the winter after a trailing job in Montana, were more than enough.

This was Belly Day. A day meant for lying indoors, belly-to-belly with a good warm woman. Outside, pellets of frigid moisture plunked harmlessly against the log cabin's shake-shingled roof. Indoors, coffee and stew simmered atop a radiant cast-iron stove. Two people managed to get even warmer atop the feather mattress that adorned a brass bedstead.

"Oh, Skye Fargo. There is so much of you. And yet I cannot get my fill."

Her words were spoken softly with just a trace of a Hungarian accent. The soft sounds came as a pleasant interruption to the tall, muscular man who'd been sitting up in bed, looking out the cabin's sole window.

The Trailsman shifted, exchanging the dismal view for one of the most exquisite faces he'd ever encountered. Her delicate visage was framed by blond hair that tumbled in riotous curls to her shoulders, glowing like desert sunshine. When she smiled, which was often, her thin lips expanded and took on a ruby hue. Dimples appeared in her creamy cheeks. Above her pert nose, deep-set blue eyes sparkled with anticipation as she joined Fargo in sitting up.

For a moment, Fargo's eyes moved downward to savor her melonlike breasts. Each was crowned with a nipple that looked like a ripe wild cherry, but tasted much sweeter. With a blush that spread from her face downward, she pulled a soft cotton bedsheet up to cover her scenery. She extended her right hand to knead Fargo's scarred shoulder.

Women were like that, he mused, while enjoying the way her soft hand warmed and soothed his flesh. No matter how friendly they'd just been with a man, women always acted embarrassed and pulled something over themselves when they sat up. Perhaps that just added to the pleasure, since his lake-blue eyes moved back to her animated face while the sheet gave him something to slide his hands under.

Her smile grew even broader as Fargo's questing hands found her breasts beneath the thin sheet. He cupped each one, sliding his thumbs over the nipples. His fingers traced across the smooth skin. He increased the pressure while she responded in kind. The sheet forgotten, her left hand rose to Fargo's other shoulder and she pulled him toward her.

The big man paused only to sweep the sheet out of the way. Their tongues met for an extended, exuberant kiss. When he came up for air, he moved down, flicking at her neck before suckling at her right nipple. When he moved to the left, she was in constant motion below him, arching up and down in a rhythm made audible by her hungry panting.

"Now, Skye, now," she urged. "Do not waste any more time."

Her taut legs spread to encircle Fargo's waist with dry warmth as he slid forward, his throbbing staff finding her wet warmth all on its own.

"Oh, that is right, that is so right," she murmured, unhooking her ankles and planting them on the mattress to give herself better leverage. Perhaps half as big as Fargo, she needed it in order to thrust upward and take in his plunges.

Automatically, he reached for a pillow to put under her bobbing rear. She caught the motion and shook her head, curls flying. "It is better this way. You should not have to do all the work."

What they were doing didn't seem like work at all to the Trailsman, but the lady could use some help. He slid his hands from her breasts to her ribs, then around to the small of her back. Grasping a firm buttock with each hand, he began pulling her to him with each deepening stroke.

He was just about there when her knees came down. She extended each limb, then slowly sidled each leg so that it was wedged between Fargo and the mattress. Her action cost him some penetration as her legs came closer together. But her back continued to oscillate, her tight moist depths rising to meet each of Fargo's slowing thrusts.

"It feels so good," she breathed, "to have so much of you pressed against me. And I have already as much of you in me as I need."

Fargo liked the sensation of thighs against thighs, and just kept pushing. Her pale skin, growing pinker by the moment, provided visible evidence of what he could already feel with every nerve in his body—she was ready.

And so was he. In a moment of mutual glory, they exploded against each other. His eruption, deep inside her, set off a shuddering reaction of ecstatic moans and her arms clutched him even tighter.

Relieved and spent, Fargo held her against him, even after rolling off. With his back to the rough log wall behind the bed and under the window, he peered over her golden curls to examine the cabin's interior by cold light of day. They'd been in such a hurry last night that he hadn't seen much before she snuffed the coal-oil lamp and jumped into bed.

His Colt, menacing in its waxed holster, sat close at hand. The heavy leather gunbelt hung uneasily around one of the brass knobs at the head of the bedstead. Sitting up a little more, Fargo spied his high-topped boots on the whipsawed plank floor. As best as he could tell without actually getting up, the right one still had the sewn-in sheath that held and hid his razor-sharp throwing knife.

Most of his possibles, including his Sharps carbine, were still down at the livery stable. The other clothes he'd had on last night—the heavy wool coat, tight blue denim trousers and a heavy checkered flannel shirt, as well as his balbriggans and thick wool socks—sat in a heap next to the boots.

The short but statuesque lady who was now sleeping comfortably next to him had been a trifle neater. At the far end of the bed was a straight-backed wooden chair. Her violet gown, ankle-length with a low sweet-heart neckline, hung over its back. Her underthings and silk stockings lay on its seat. Under the rungs sat shiny patent-leather dancing shoes.

What made the shoes stand out were the low heels, which sparkled even in the gray mournful light that grudgingly seeped through the window. The heels were silver, solid silver.

Fargo had first noticed those flashing heels last night. After too many nights without either, he'd started looking for a dry bed and hot meal. His first stop was Fairplay, a mining camp right on the edge of the vast, mountain-rimmed valley called South Park. One hotel had a vacant room, but both livery stables were full up.

"That big Ovaro of yours is a splendid critter," a

young hostler commented, "and I'm sure you take good care of him."

After Fargo's nod, the stablehand said there'd likely be room to spare up at Buckskin Joe. A decent wagon road covered the nine miles up a steep-walled gulch.

The boy had been right. Not only could a man find a decent livery stable in Buckskin Joe, he could find most everything else, decent or indecent: blacksmith and butcher shops, restaurants, bakeries, billiard rooms, four hotels, halls that featured minstrel shows and traveling actors, one big whorehouse on the edge of town, and at least a dozen saloons, most with entertainment.

Fargo had strolled into Billy Buck's Saloon last night after making sure the Ovaro would be tended. Shortly after warming his innards with a steak and some whiskey, he'd seen the night's entertainment—a pretty gal singing and dancing while an old-timer beat on an out-of-tune piano. The miners stomped their feet during her songs. After each tune, they tossed coins toward the tiny stage.

Her shining, expressive face and her plaintive voice were enough to make any man remember her wistfully. But it was the silver-heeled dancing shoes that gave her the only name anyone knew her by: Silver Heels.

Even in the glare of the hissing limelights during her performance, Silver Heels had noticed the newcomer, the tall man with the full beard. His jet-black hair hung to his broad shoulders. He hardly moved at all, but when he did, the motions were sudden and precise. He never looked nervous, but folks around him tended to get edgy. Although the barroom was crowded, the miners gave him a wide berth. He had a table to himself.

Afterward, when the other patrons had settled down to serious drinking and gambling, one thing had led to another. And, well, there they were, up in her cabin on this gloomy, overcast, drizzly morning.

Fargo released Silver Heels. She was lying there so contentedly that if she'd been a cat, she would have been purring. She might even have purred loud enough to overcome the ground-shaking thunder that rose from

13

the thumping stamps of the recently erected Pioneer Quartz Mill down at the edge of Buckskin Joe.

The Trailsman sat up and glanced out the window again. Did this spell of bleak weather mean that winter was off to a more vicious start than usual this year? Or would the clouds lift in time for the traditional few weeks of Indian summer?

Either way, there wouldn't be much he could do about it except get to a more sensible place, like southern Texas. The Trailsman sighed and looked for his wide-brimmed hat. He had to edge his way over Silver Heels and pull his long legs out from under the warm blankets before he found it, under the bed next to a porcelain chamber pot.

Like most men who spent a lot of time outdoors, the Trailsman dressed from the top down. Hat first, then shirt, then trousers, and finally boots. He was just tugging them on when Silver Heels stirred.

"Skye, honey, where are you going?"

Fargo bristled, the way he always did whenever a woman asked that question. But he calmed himself. After a deep, slow breath, the Trailsman answered, "Into town to check on my Ovaro. And on my other gear."

"And after that?"

"Guess that depends."

"Depends on what?"

"On where I feel like going. And on where I feel welcome."

"You ought to know that you are always welcome here."

He turned to stare at her dreamy face, enjoying the way her long natural eyelashes batted like frolicsome butterflies.

"I guess I should know that." He smiled. "Are you going somewhere?"

"Someday," she sighed. "Someday I shall be dancing and singing in Denver. And in New Orleans and San Francisco and St. Louis and Philadelphia. Perhaps even in New York. Or in Paris and London."

"What's stopping you now? Why not go for the big time? Why are you entertaining a bunch of tired, drunk miners in a little town in the middle of nowhere?" Fargo rose and stepped over to the stove, where he found a tin cup and filled it with hot coffee.

"For my career. It must start someplace," Silver Heels explained.

"But I've seen the singers and dancers in big cities." Fargo sipped at the scalding coffee, holding the hot metal cup gingerly by its handle. "Believe me, honey, you're better than most of the competition."

"I have heard such." She looked as though she intended to sit up. Then she changed her mind and lay back on her side. "But a girl who goes to the city? She must sing in a chorus. She must dance with a troupe. If fortune favors her, she becomes an understudy."

"At least you'd be getting somewhere," Fargo consoled. "You shouldn't be wasting your talent around here. Those boys whistle and stomp whenever they see a gal, any gal. The only talent she needs is a low bodice or a short skirt." He glanced appreciatively at the sinuous form the blankets took with her beneath them. "Not that you're shy any of those talents."

Silver Heels's laughter came from low in her throat. "That is true."

The laughter ceased. Her face hardened before she continued. "When I perform, Mr. Fargo, I am the only one on the stage. And I do like these miners."

He didn't quite know how to answer that, so he didn't. Some folks liked being big frogs in small puddles. And if the stagestruck Silver Heels played her cards right, she probably could continue being the star as her career progressed. She sure had the looks. Her stage performance still had a few rough edges, but she had natural talent. Enough practice in these backwoods barrooms and she might indeed draw packed houses in London someday.

Silver Heels returned Fargo's smile with one of her own, then settled back to sleep. He drained the coffee, then used the cup to dip some stew. Out on the covered porch, which ran the full breadth of her cabin, the Trailsman buttoned his knee-length wool coat tight. He cursed the need for it, then wrapped his form in an

15

ungainly yellow mackintosh. After gulping the warm stew, he sloshed down the hillside to town.

It couldn't have been more than a quarter mile. But by the time Fargo saw his Ovaro, he was jealous. The big pinto stallion looked almost sassy. He was standing sleek and dry in his warm stall, munching on oats from a bucket.

The Ovaro's owner didn't much like oats, but he took considerable pleasure in feeling dry. This bone-chilling damp came right through the rubberized cloak. The big wool coat underneath didn't slow it down worth mention, either.

Looking for an excuse to stay under a roof for as long as he could, Fargo asked where the post office was. He figured on sitting next to a red-hot potbellied stove. Then he could take his time composing and writing notes to some acquaintances in sunny San Antonio. They were expecting him, more or less, one of these days.

"It's the general store, too," a short, swarthy stable-hand explained. "Just down a few doors. Right across from the bank."

Fargo picked his way along the deserted, muddy street, examining signs through the drizzle that was starting to become sleet. The false front across the ruts and puddles announced that the flimsy building held the "Bank of Buckskin Joe." But when he turned his head and looked up, he saw that he was standing in front of the "United States Post Office. Laurette, Colorado."

He scraped his boot soles against a convenient rock and hurried inside. "Anybody mind telling me where I am?" he asked.

None of the four idlers swapping lies by the stove and the cracker barrel saw fit to enlighten the Trails-man. The man behind the counter, a fellow whose big brow looked even bigger because he was going bald, waited for Fargo to shake the water off his slicker before answering.

"You can take your choice, mister." The storekeeper's salt-and-pepper soup-strainer mustache twitched before he went on. "Everybody calls this place Buckskin, or Buckskin Joe, 'cept for the government. They say we get our mail at Laurette."

Happy to be warm, Fargo just stood there, shaking his head. So the stoop-shouldered man continued. "Don't exactly know why. Happened a while back, I reckon, and we just moved over here from Oro City. Nobody ever asked before." He turned to the door that led to the back room and hollered back to ask his wife, Augusta, if she had any good explanation.

The tiny woman wore her dark hair in a bun. Gold-rimmed spectacles bobbed atop her chiseled nose as she came through the door, bearing several parcels but no answers. Her husband stepped around the counter and approached Fargo, ready to make friends.

He stuck out his hand. "Name's Hod Tabor, stranger. I'm the postmaster and mayor."

Before Fargo could shake hands and introduce himself, he heard sloshing out in the street. The Trailsman instantly turned to stare silently through the store's front windows. It was doleful dark outside, and the lanterns were lit inside. He needed a few seconds to ignore the reflections and see what was really out there.

Four horsemen clad in yellow slickers had just pulled up to the bank. Two were on their way through its front door. One man stayed in his saddle, holding the other horses' reins. The other outside man had dismounted. He held a rifle and warily surveyed the soggy street.

Fargo reached into his slicker and pulled out his Colt before turning to the others in the room.

They stared at him, glazed-eyed and petrified. "If you all stay low," the Trailsman announced, "you'll likely be safe. Your bank's getting robbed."

Fargo dropped immediately into a crouch, a pickle barrel at his back as he peeked out the window. He heard shuffling feet, all bound for such safety as could be found behind the counter, or maybe even the back room. Staring across the street, he studied on his next step.

Taking out at least one of the outside men wouldn't be that difficult. He could probably get them both.

17

But the inside men would hear the shots. They'd be forted up inside the bank, with lead flying every which way. Fargo had never met a banker so innocent that the man didn't deserve some grief. But in those situations, you couldn't tell who might get hurt. It was at least possible that somebody honest was inside the bank.

Better to wait until the two came out, and get them all at once.

Alert for any motion through the bank's doors, Fargo felt his tension rising. Just how long could it take two men to wave their guns, present a sack, and get some clerk to fill it with money?

He wasn't the only one who was getting impatient. One of the local loafers huddled behind the counter shouted, "Hey, what's going on?"

"Stay down and stay quiet if you don't want to end up hurt," Fargo intoned. There was enough going to happen any second in front of him. He didn't want to have to worry about what might be going on behind him.

After an eternity, the bank doors began to open. Fargo reined his eagerness until he could be sure. Two yellow slickers. Two drawn guns. One bulging, heavy gunnysack. The Trailsman didn't need any more confirmation.

But he waited until the double doors slammed shut behind the two robbers. No sense giving the bastards any easy way to duck back.

The sadiron Fargo had been holding in his left hand smashed the thin pane of glass he'd been looking through.

The Trailsman's steady Colt barked. The horse holder rocked back in his saddle as a bullet smashed past his rib cage. He slumped forward as the lead emerged from his back after plowing through his vital organs.

But his gloved hand still clutched the reins. Fargo's second shot creased the muddy rump of the horse holder's dapple-gray mare. She found it annoying as hell and reared up, tossing her bleeding rider into the mud. He dropped all the reins as he fell. His mount took off down the street, running faster than some horses Fargo had bet money on. The three other mud-splattered horses instantly decided that they'd rather be somewhere else.

The rifle-toting robber saw his getaway hopes vanishing into the drizzle. Without taking time to aim, he snapped off one shot toward the post office and lit out down the street. It wasn't a bad shot, considering. A pane just above Fargo's head shattered, spraying jagged chunks of glass.

Fargo felt his own blood pouring onto his neck. He ignored the warm, oozy sensation and rolled toward the door. Staying prone, he nudged it open with the butt of his left hand.

The moving door drew a barrage of pistol shots from the two remaining robbers. Through the crack between the door and its frame, Fargo saw powder smoke rising from down the street. They had to be crouched behind the horse trough that stood next door to the bank.

He slithered forward, hoping for a better view. Blood was getting into his eyes now. He brought his left arm forward and wiped at his face. The rubbery coating of the mackintosh didn't wipe blood worth mention. He shook his head to clear his eyes, and wasn't even sure that he had. Everything looked so dim, dim even for this dreary, overcast morning.

The Trailsman's Colt wasn't being held by a steady hand anymore, he noticed. He clutched its grips with both big hands, his arms stretched before him as he lay on his belly. Fargo focused his attention on that horse trough.

Moments later, a hat poked up. Fargo held until he was sure there was a head under it.

Fargo's shot went a trifle low. His soft lead bullet sailed into the thin planking that formed the trough's brim. The wood deformed the projectile, and a nail deflected it slightly. Fargo's .44-caliber slug was disk-shaped when it hit the surface of the water at an extremely low angle.

Like a stone being tossed by a boy at a pond's edge, the whirling saucer of lead skipped off the water's surface. Its sharp spinning edge hit the robber just where the brim of his hat met his head. A flurry of brains, hair, skull, and blood erupted from under the dripping Stetson.

The Trailsman couldn't be sure just how he'd ended that bank robber's career as he slithered forward. Smoke from his shot, combined with the blood that kept filling his eyes, made it too difficult to see clearly. He felt his elbows sinking into the mud.

Pulling himself onward through the gelid muck, Fargo shook the blood out of his eyes and got a clear fix on the trough again. He pulled up on his hands to be sure he could shoot when the time came.

Down the street, there were shots. Five or six of them, their sharp reports muffled by the drizzle. The citizens of Buckskin Joe must have gotten excited by now, for Fargo heard closer shots. Shots right behind him, in fact, as he saw the fool behind the horse trough decide to make a break. It was just a blur of hazy gray motion.

Fargo gritted his teeth. Squeezing a trigger had never before taken such effort. Nonetheless, he managed. And then he couldn't see.

The next thing Fargo noticed was the aroma of fresh-baked bread. At first he couldn't be positive that it wasn't part of a dream, considering the trouble he had sitting up and making sure he was awake.

He looked around. He could tell he was sitting on a cot of some sort. Wherever he was, the room was shadowy, except for where a shaft of brilliant sunlight came through a high, tiny window. Fargo shook his head some more and looked toward the bread aroma.

A hoopskirted woman stood there, holding a wicker basket, its contents covered by a linen towel. The only problem was that row of iron bars that stood between him and her.

Fargo looked behind her. There was a table out there, covered with papers, with an empty chair before it. The middle of the anteroom was dominated by an immense potbellied stove, as tall as the woman.

As for his end of the building, one wall was bars, and the other three were foot-thick logs. The sole window had bars, and it was a good ten feet off the splintery plank floor.

He was in jail. And he had company. The robber who'd been holding the rifles was atop the room's other cot, snoring away under a rough wool blanket.

Hoping that this was a dream, but knowing better, Fargo finally spoke. "You'd be Mrs. Tabor?"

The woman nodded. "And who might you be?" she asked.

Fargo put his bare feet on the floor and stood up. It gave him giddy, dizzy feelings, but he fought them off.

"Does it matter?" he asked, taking his time for the six or eight steps from his cot to the bars.

"I'm afraid it probably doesn't." Through a gap between the bars, she extended her small but work-hardened right hand. The thin red lines on her thumb and forefinger evidenced many hours of needlework. Those callused knuckles came from washing tons of laundry with a scrub board. What most interested Fargo, though, were the two steaming rolls, dripping with butter, that she dropped into his grateful hand.

"I imagine I know why," he said before nibbling at the roll. The bread tasted exquisite, and he wanted to prolong his pleasure, savor every moment of it.

"It's not right," she said. "I know you were not part of that bank robbery. I am absolutely certain that I saw only four horses out there before you commenced firing."

The bread wasn't going down easy because Fargo's throat felt so dry. He managed to swallow a bit before answering. "You're absolutely right, ma'am. So what am I doing in jail?"

"Because the menfolk here think you were part of the gang. You came into our store just before the robbery. You were wearing a yellow mackintosh, just like the others. You told us all to stay low just when the robbery started. Nobody knows who you are or where you came from."

Fargo's throat got even drier as he took another bite from the delicious biscuit. She didn't wait for him to reply before she went on.

"I know you were shooting at those outlaws, that

21

the only reason we still have our hard-earned savings is because you saw the robbery and acted immediately to stop them before they rode off."

Fargo nodded and managed to choke out a few words. "That's pretty much how it all happened, ma'am."

She stiffened and straightened her back. "I told them so. But when they all ran out there after the smoke settled, they were sure that they were the ones who'd shot up that gang. And there you were, lying out on the street, bleeding. That was all they needed to know."

Fargo knew better, but asked anyway. "Won't there be a trial, Mrs. Tabor?"

Her chiseled features became even more granite-like. "Before a miner's court. Where my husband, Horace, will be the judge. He's not a bad man, nor a mean one. But this is a man's world. Who would listen to me, even if I were permitted to testify?"

No matter how good that biscuit tasted, it was sure hard to swallow when a man's mouth was so parched. Fargo swirled his tongue around and mustered enough moisture so that he could talk without stumbling too much.

"No, ma'am, and those miner's courts don't waste much time carrying out their sentences." The words were coming easier now. "I don't see why they bothered to bandage me up if they're fixing to hang me."

Augusta Tabor's hazel eyes drew into points. "They didn't. I did."

Fargo rubbed the bandage on the back of his head thoughtfully. He felt another on his right shoulder, and noticed at least three on his left arm. He'd caught several pieces of glass. It wasn't any wonder that he'd nearly bled to death.

"Well, Mrs. Tabor, I surely do thank you for that. Not many jailers that considerate."

A hint of a smile crossed her face. "It may seem that the Tabors hold all the offices around here, but I am not the town jailer. That would be Pete Green. He comes by here several times a day, to make sure there's a fire in the stove."

"Then what brings you by with these hot biscuits?"

She drew her back even straighter as she stared straight at him. "Because I am a decent and civilized God-fearing woman. And I believe that civilization and Christianity mean that we must extend decency to everyone. Which includes men in jail. Or we are no better than the savages we complain about."

Fargo looked at his remaining biscuit before meeting her stare. "Mrs. Tabor, I've heard plenty of talk along those lines. But you're the first person that's ever bothered to make actions suit the words." He swallowed hard and pointed toward his snoring cellmate. "Should I save this for him?"

Augusta Tabor shook her head and handed him several more biscuits. "Eat all you can. As soon as I finish serving luncheon to our boarders, I'll come back by with some leftovers." She turned and walked out. Fargo stared at her back, kind of surprised that she didn't sport wings. No halo, either.

Sitting back on his cot, Fargo had almost finished the second biscuit when his cellmate awoke, sitting up and rubbing his eyes.

Towheaded and lanky, he looked startled when he saw Fargo.

"Didn't know that you'd ever come around," he finally muttered.

"Don't see that it matters all that much to be awake for my own hanging," Fargo grunted back.

"It's sure the shits, ain't it." The voice was thin, reedy, nasal. He wasn't much more than a boy who'd just started shaving regular. "Told them assholes that you was on their side, not mine. It's a caution how folks won't listen to you when you've just been robbin' their bank."

Fargo leaned back against the rough wall. "I've noticed." He scratched his back against a chunk of bark. "Just how long we been in here, anyway?"

"Four days, I think. You had the right idea, sleepin'. Ain't much else to do in here, 'cept wait for the weather to clear some so they can all get to town for the big hanging."

The shaft of sunshine looked worse than all those days of gray drizzle. Fargo tossed the man a biscuit.

"Mrs. Tabor's been by this morning, I see. Can't figure this place out. She come in and took care of you, brings us food, an' her man's the one that's gonna point us to the noose. I've got it comin', but you don't."

Fargo stood up and stretched. "Hell, boy, nobody thinks he's got that comin'."

"But I do," the lad protested. "We for damn sure meant to rob that bank afore you started shootin'. Not that it mattered all that much even if you'd been somewhere else. Ol' Griswold would've got his money back."

"Griswold would be the banker?"

"'Bout the best you can say of that double-dealing sack of buffalo chips. Might as well get strung up young. Can't be much worse'n spendin' my whole life workin' to pay that bastard Rufus Griswold. Either way I end up with nothin'."

Still feeling a mite addled every time he took a step, Fargo sat back down. One set of confusion at a time was enough. "It's not like I have to believe it or anything, kid. But why don't you tell me the whole damn story? As you noticed, there ain't a lot else to do in here except sleep, and I've got my fill of that for a spell."

The kid said his name was Jim Sedgwick. He had an older brother, Red, one of the men who'd entered the bank. They and their two cousins, Will and Sam Cockburn, the other robbers, had grown up on neighboring ranches on the Kansas prairies. When the talk of gold in the Rockies spread in 1859, they'd naturally headed west in hopes of adventure and easy money.

"Come to find out, we was raised cow an' didn't know shit from wild honey 'bout mining," Jim explained. "But, hell, them miners likes thick beefsteaks for dinner, just like everybody else."

Fargo nodded while the boy scratched at himself.

"An' there was oxen aplenty. Scraggly critters that make tough, stringy beef after pullin' wagons here." The brothers and cousins discovered they could buy worn-out oxen for ten or twenty dollars a head from new arrivals. After a few months of grazing high meadows or native hay, one fattened ox fetched upward of ninety dollars.

"So we had us a good deal. Found us a fair ranch, few miles down the Arkansas from Oro City right under the Twin Lakes. We done filed on it with the government land office, an' figgered we was in the cow business. Even when them Oro City placers pretty well petered out last summer, there was plenty of other minin' camps hereabouts. Ain't all that much trouble to trail cattle when they're payin' good money somewhere."

There had been a time when a young Skye Fargo had thought that trailing cattle was a glorious adventure, rather than just a dusty job, but he didn't intrude on the boy's story. "So how'd you folks enter the banking business?"

"Hell, it come to us. We was goin' good for a couple years, an' then ol' Rufus Griswold shows up on the porch one mornin'. He's got the Lake County sheriff at his side, an' both of 'em are grinnin' like shit-eatin' hounds."

"Let me guess," Fargo interrupted. "Griswold had some paper that showed your ranch land was part of some big placer claim that he'd foreclosed on. So you could come up with some instant money, or he'd take over your ranch."

"You called that dead right," the young cowhand agreed. "Ten thousand dollars we was supposed to come up with afore the first of November. We scared up five of it fast, sellin' cattle in a hurry. But no, ol' Griswold wasn't gonna cut us no slack. Ten thousand by November, or we was out of our ranch."

"Try seein' a lawyer?" Fargo asked.

The kid laughed. "Shee-it," he spat. "You know, you can allus tell when some mining camp is about to run outta gold. All the lawyers leave. Only one left over there, an' he's Griswold's man."

Griswold, the boy explained, owned not just the bank in Oro City, but he'd bought out Tabor's store when that merchant had given up on the place and moved over to Buckskin Joe, a more promising camp. The two towns sat only sixteen miles apart. But that didn't tell the whole story, since they were separated by the Mosquito Range, a wall of mountains that never dipped less than 13,000 feet above sea level.

Not that that bothered Griswold, since he also owned the bank in Buckskin Joe, as well as the bank down in Fairplay, and another just across a spur of the Tenmile Range, over in Breckenridge.

"Sounded so sensible a couple days ago," the boy mused aloud. "We could just ride over Mosquito Pass an' withdraw some money from Griswold's bank here. Day was perfect for it, nobody on the street or nothin'. No shit, we didn't want nobody to get hurt. Then we was gonna scat back home with the money. We could sit on it a bit an' let ol' Griswold's mouth start waterin' just thinkin' about how he was gonna screw some more hard-workin' folks. Just afore he fixed to take our land, we was gonna ride in an' pay him in gold. With his own damn money."

The boy's forced laughter began to choke, and Fargo saw his wide brown eyes moisten. But the cowboy wouldn't let himself cry, even though sobs interrupted the rest of his story.

"You knows how it turned out, mister. Part of it, anyhow. Sam an' Red was both married up. Sam had a little boy, an' Red's wife has got one comin' soon. We told 'em we was just goin' off to buy some worn-out trail oxen."

Fargo stepped over and draped an arm across the young man's lean but muscular shoulders. The kid swallowed hard and tried to pretend that there weren't tears running down his tanned face.

"Was never my intention to put your family in Boot Hill, kid. An' it don't seem fair at all that banks can rob you an' get away with it."

The kid nodded agreement as Fargo continued. "But look at it some other ways. Mrs. Tabor's a fine woman that must work damn hard for such money as she's able to put by. And when you robbed that bank, you were taking her savings just as much as you were pulling one on Rufus Griswold."

The boy sputtered some before answering. "Mister, I never said what we done was right. What was done to us wasn't right, neither. An' what's bein' done to you is a cryin' shame. But it ain't gonna matter none. By this time tomorrow, likely, they'll have us done tried and hanged."

Fargo stood and examined their cell. "It does look like breaking out of here might be a problem. Don't suppose either of us has an ax along." Before he could continue, the front door opened.

The man who came in limped. He had a game arm, too. His belly protruded over the belt of his baggy twill trousers. Behind his full beard, he was working on a chaw of tobacco. Some of that was running down his beard and spilling onto his faded corduroy shirt. The man obviously wasn't fit for anything else, so he had to be Pete Green, the jailer.

"See both you bastards finally got up," he grumped.

Nobody bothered to tell him he was right.

With a vacant, moronic expression, Green drooled and stared at them. Fargo decided the man was as stupid as he looked, and whispered to Jim Sedgwick as he sat down on the cot next to the would-be bank robber.

Sedgwick's eyes grew wide at Fargo's suggestion, but he grudgingly whispered agreement. Even if Fargo's notion was risky as hell, it beat just sitting in there, waiting for the noose to arrive.

2

Pete Green sullenly shoved several chunks of wood into the stove and adjusted its drafts and damper. He spat, getting the bulk of his stream into the crusted spittoon by the table. Most of the rest dripped into a crack between the planks. The jailer turned to look in again at Fargo and Jim Sedgwick.

"Trial's tomorrow, boys. I hopes you dance good at the end of a rope. Lotsa folks comin' in for the show."

Fargo just leered back while planting his arm across his cellmate's shoulders. The Sedgwick kid presented a sick, frightened expression, like a wounded doe's. "Mr. Green," he begged, "can't you find no other place to keep me. This feller here, he's, uh . . . well, he's kinda funny."

Green laughed without humor, then worked his chaw over to the other cheek. "Ain't me that picked who you was gonna rob banks with, boy. Now, quit pesterin' me. Mrs. Tabor'll be by with your lunch shortly." The jailer turned and shuffled toward the door.

Outside, he had barely gotten the plank door pulled shut behind him when he heard an awful scream. Then another, along with sounds of thrashing bodies. He muttered something about the low type of men they were getting in jail these days, and turned on his good leg.

From the doorway, Green saw Fargo's big left hand clamped over his lean cellmate's mouth. The kid's cheeks and eyes were fixing to pop any second. He kicked and struggled to reach the bars. More or less crawling on his hands and knees, Sedgwick wasn't getting far. He had to drag Fargo as he struggled.

The Trailsman hunkered over him, almost covering

him from behind. Once Fargo saw that the jailer had returned, he released some of the pressure on Sedgwick's mouth. With his other hand, he jerked the kid's bony right arm into a hammerlock.

Flailing with his free hand, Sedgwick collapsed to the floor. "Jesus, help me, mister," he shouted. "This crazy man's fixin' to cornhole me."

To help him make the point, Fargo grabbed at the waistband of the cowboy's denim jeans.

"You cut that out," the jailer hollered. "We don't allow no crimes against nature in our jail."

Fargo just ignored the order. A manic gleam sparkled in his lake-blue eyes. Twisting and writhing, Sedgwick rolled out from under the Trailsman, heading for the bars.

Fargo leaped up from behind, grabbing the boy's shoulders and slamming him forward against the bars at the corner, where the bars and wall came together, several paces down from the door. His prey clutched the iron barriers and kicked back like an angry mule. Fargo sidestepped and put on the most lustful smile he could muster. With one hand, he grabbed a shank of the cowboy's brown hair. With the other, he reached for his own trousers and began to unbutton the fly.

The horrified jailer finally got around to acting. Fargo felt relieved that their charade didn't need to go any further, because he was running out of ideas. And he didn't feel too comfortable as it was.

But he maintained his lusty leer and manic gleam, acting as though he didn't even notice that Pete Green had managed to unlock the cell door. Took the man long enough, the way his hands shook. Likely that was because he used his game arm to fumble with the key. The other held a rusty crowbar that had to be at least a yard long.

With the crowbar clutched in both hands, Green approached warily. Fargo leaned forward to Sedgwick, his face next to the cowboy's ear. "Just a second here," he whispered. "Two more steps."

Green took the two shaky steps and began to raise his club. He had hopes of braining the huge pervert who was fixing to molest the hapless young prisoner.

"Now," Fargo whispered. Releasing Sedgwick, he spun around on the balls of his feet to dodge the jailer's clumsy upward swing.

Fargo went high, and Sedgwick went low. Fargo's big arm swung down. His hammerlike fist slammed into the jailer's good arm. Jerking it back in fiery pain, the man let go of the crowbar.

As it fell, the bar's claw end just missed Sedgwick, who had turned and dived for the jailer's knees. His flying tackle brought the jailer down, a process aided by Fargo's roundhouse left to the man's jaw.

Fargo didn't even mind that the punch had caused a spouting geyser of tobacco juice to spray his face. Wiping his face with his sleeve, he surveyed the cell.

Sedgwick was up, standing next to the sprawled body of Pete Green. The cowboy looked as if he was having a hard time resisting his natural temptation to kick the jailer. Fargo, too, felt tempted. But he didn't act. After all, there were times, and this was one of them, that Fargo was grateful that there were so many stupid, mean people in the world.

Instead, he headed for their cell door, Sedgwick right behind him. With the key he'd borrowed from the knocked-out jailer, Fargo locked the man in behind them.

Next to the flimsy table by the front door sat several wooden beer cases. Fargo flung the hinged top of one up, and didn't recognize the boots and coat stuffed inside. But Sedgwick did, and Fargo's goods were in the next box.

While they tugged on their boots, Fargo asked if Sedgwick had any idea where their guns were.

"Likely in the sheriff's office," he answered, his voice turning glum when he added, "it's right across the goddamn street."

Fargo peeked out the door. Sure enough, it was broad daylight, and they were right in town. He realized he should have known that all along. Their whole building vibrated constantly from the steady thump of the stamp mill.

The Trailsman decided he hadn't noticed the ongoing rumble because it had been there all the time he'd been out, as well as when he woke up. He'd just gotten so accustomed to it that he would have noticed the sound only if it had stopped. A man who lived by his senses couldn't afford to have any of them dulled. It was just another irksome thing about towns.

But the most irksome thing right now was how busy the street was. There were a few wagons, but mostly men on horseback. Hardly anybody walked.

As Fargo watched, a man rode up to the front of a haberdasher's and hollered. The storekeeper came out into the warm sunshine of Indian summer and hollered something back. The rider nodded. Moments later, the storekeeper came back out, bearing three wrapped parcels that he handed to his mounted customer. The man handed him some money and rode off.

Damn convenient, Fargo thought. You could do all your trading here and never get off your horse. But having all those folks on the street meant that escaping from the jail building might be harder than getting out of their jail cell.

He turned to his companion. "You got any ideas?"

"Mister, I can't even rob a bank without gettin' caught. How the hell would I know how to bust loose from jail?"

"Got a point there," Fargo conceded. "If it was dark, gettin' out of here wouldn't be much of a problem. Way it is, the damn sheriff is probably sitting over there, with nothing better to do than watch this door."

Fargo felt his stomach sink when he peeked out the door again. Augusta Tabor was approaching from only a few yards away, toting a lunch-filled lard bucket in each hand. Fargo eased the door shut and stepped back. He'd never been one to take hostages. Now it didn't look as though he had much choice.

It would be one thing if Mrs. Tabor had been as snooty as she looked in her hoopskirt and spectacles. But she was one of those hard-working, pleasant women who gave decency a good name.

After setting down the lard buckets, she pushed the door open, picked them up, and came through, stepping briskly. Before her eyes could adjust from the bright street to the dim interior, Sedgwick had the door slammed shut behind her.

She looked back at Pete Green, still sprawled on the cell floor before turning to her left, where Fargo stood. Her face showed some surprise, but absolutely no fear.

"Oh dear," she said, shaking her head. "Do you still want your lunch?"

She didn't look nearly as flabbergasted as Fargo felt. "I could use some, ma'am," he finally answered. From behind her, Sedgwick voiced his agreement.

"Then don't let me bother you. Go ahead and eat. I'll wait, just as I always do. It's my only chance to sit down, all day." She set the buckets down and moved over toward the chair.

"Don't this bother you none?" Sedgwick asked as she spread her skirts and sat.

"Your trial and hanging would have bothered me more," she said in a crisp, educated voice. "The entire affair is a travesty of justice. Bank robbery is hardly a capital offense." She turned to face Fargo. "And you, sir, were gravely injured while preventing the robbery. Yet people are already coming into town for tomorrow's announced activities."

Fargo swallowed a big bite of roast-beef sandwich before replying. "Those activities being the trial and so forth?"

She nodded. "My Horace was so excited, too. Anything that draws a crowd to town is good for business. And he so enjoys having an audience when he's the judge. Believe me, he would have tried to give you as fair a trial as possible."

Sedgwick had been gobbling his sandwich, but he found time to rephrase his first question. "Mrs. Tabor, aren't you worried at all, in here with two escaped prisoners?"

The short woman leaned back in her chair, then stiffened and turned. "Perhaps. But, young man, I'll have you know that Horace and I settled in Kansas when the Jayhawkers and the Free-Soilers were at war, and our son Maxcy was just a baby. Many's the night that I sat up next to his cradle, sure that our homestead would be raided and burned."

As they worked on their fried potatoes in silence, she went on. "Horace decided he'd had enough, so we crossed the prairie in a covered wagon. Along the way, the Kiowa attacked. They held me captive for two days until I was rescued."

She lowered her eyes and Fargo knew better than to ask about those two days.

"And ever since, we've lived in these rough-and-tumble mining camps where murder and mayhem are almost commonplace. Auraria, then Russell Gulch, Oro City, and now here. I've ridden stagecoaches that were robbed. After all that, I suppose there isn't much that can frighten me. What happens will happen."

"But at least you and your man seem to be getting somewhere," Sedgwick commented. Fargo hoped the cowboy wouldn't start his own hard-luck story. The hope was rewarded as Augusta asked how that was so.

"You've got a busy store," the young man said. "And he's the postmaster and mayor and all. You board folks and take in laundry and all that. You an' Mr. Tabor ought to be doing right well."

Augusta huffed before answering. "We ought to be. But my Horace never turns a deaf ear to a prospector. He'll grubstake any fool with a gold pan and a claim, no matter how unlikely the prospects. He keeps telling me that someday one of them will strike it rich. I think we'd be better off just saving what we work so hard to earn." She sighed. "But does he ever listen to me?"

Fargo polished of the fist-sized piece of chocolate cake, then asked what she intended to do about the jailbreak in front of her.

"If I do not return to our store soon," she said, "Horace will be perturbed. And who's to say what might happen if the mayor . . ."

"Say no more, ma'am," the Trailsman interrupted. "What I wondered was whether you planned to mention that him and me are out here while Pete Green is in there."

She smiled. "Even if I did, I very much doubt that they would listen. The menfolk refused to believe me when I insisted that you were not part of the robbery. Since they're so sure that they can handle this matter without hearing what I have to say, I suppose I can let them."

The diminutive Mrs. Tabor rose. Stepping briskly again, she picked up the empty lunch buckets and marched out, stopping only to open and shut the door.

"You believe her?" Sedgwick hissed. "You think she really won't say nothin'?"

Fargo nodded. Seeing that Sedgwick still looked incredulous, he emphasized his point. "I do believe her. She's a tough-minded gal whose toes have been stepped on too many times. She's taken all the guff she's going to take. Providing we get out of town real soon, she's not likely to cause us any trouble."

"But how we gonna do that?" Sedgwick asked.

Fargo still didn't have an answer. He felt annoyed, but he couldn't really blame his recent cellmate for asking.

Back behind them, Pete Green was coming around, rolling a bit while moaning low and awful. The sounds gave the Trailsman a quick notion. They could take him hostage. Fargo dismissed it just as fast. Green was such a worthless old fool that nobody would care if he got kidnapped.

Fargo edged the front door ajar and examined the street. His heart jumped into his throat when he saw the sheriff step outside and start their way. But it settled back down when he saw the bowlegged lawman turn and head on up the street. Then the sheriff followed his tarnished star through the batwing doors of the Deadfall Saloon.

The sheriff likely hadn't even wetted his lips yet with his complimentary rotgut when Fargo saw opportunity coming down the street.

It was a horse-drawn train of four high-bodied ore wagons. They'd just been emptied at the stamp mill. The freighters did their own shoveling. Since each wagon held about eight tons of rock, the wagon drivers were likely as tired and uninterested as they appeared to be.

When the last wagon came by, its huge wheels churning up dust to join the cloud the others had raised, Fargo and Sedgwick bolted out the jailhouse door.

They had to trot down the rutted street behind the wagon for a few steps before they were able to jump aboard. The tailgate was just as high as the wagon's extended sideboards, seven or eight feet off above the ground. Grabbing the top rail of the tailgate, Fargo sprang up and clambered over it, tumbling headfirst into the deep wagon bed.

As he straightened, Sedgwick's lanky frame came spilling over the tailgate. Fargo rolled up and started out of the way, only to find his path blocked by a length of tight chain that connected the sideboards, preventing them from spreading when the wagon was loaded.

So the Trailsman knew that the cowboy hadn't meant to kick him in the jaw, even if it still smarted some. Judging by how dizzy he felt after the somersault, he reckoned his body hadn't finished replacing all the blood he'd lost. But the main worry now was whether the freighter, perched up ahead of them on a cross-sprung seat, was going to notice that two men were now hunkering in his gritty wagon bed.

The matched Belgians out in front no doubt noticed they were tugging a little harder, but one of these ore wagons weighed three thousand pounds empty. Fargo and Sedgwick weren't enough to matter on that account. And since the driver's seat had its own set of transverse leaf springs, he likely blamed any bouncing he felt on the ruts on the street, if he felt much of anything after shoveling fifteen thousand pounds of rock from the wagon bed to the ore chute at the mill. From what they could judge by studying on his broad, sweat-stained back, the man seemed content to sit there and let the horses do all the thinking and working.

Fargo had at first figured on riding the wagon into the woods, then jumping out. Crouched and looking through a narrow gap between boards on the wagon wall, the Trailsman didn't see much chance of getting into the trees—ever. Although there were occasional lodgepoles and stands of aspen farther up the road, stumps dotted the nearby hillsides. Just about everything that could be converted to pit props for the mines or firewood for the miners had been cut down.

So when the massive wagon lumbered past Daisy Melrose's two-story whorehouse on the far edge of town, Fargo sprang up and vaulted over the back rail. Landing on his feet, he saw that the thoroughfare had twisted some. Several nondescript log buildings shielded him from being seen by folks in the middle of town. That made it a little easier to run over and extend a helping hand when Sedgwick landed a few yards away, in a heap of windmilling arms and legs.

They ran right around the whorehouse, headed for its backyard. Fargo spied a fair-sized woodshed that would hold them comfortable until dark. But somebody spied the two men.

3

"Hey, fellers, we're closed till after supper time." Fargo halted in his tracks to look up to see where that brassy feminine voice was coming from.

The voice belonged to a rather plain-faced gal who was shaking her shoulder-length brown curls while leaning out a second-story window. She had on a green velvet robe, but its front hung open so as to display her considerable charms. And she didn't bother to pull it shut while Fargo and Sedgwick paused to enjoy a look at some mountains far softer than those granite peaks that surrounded them.

"Just passin' through, ma'am," Fargo explained.

Before answering, she looked him up and down, the way a rancher examines a prize bull when he's at a sale. "You don't need to be in such a hurry, you big devil."

Sedgwick just stood there like a little kid looking in the front window of a candy shop.

So Fargo had to say something. "Fact is, ma'am, we do need to hurry right along." She still looked interested, so the Trailsman added, "Besides, we ain't carryin' any money."

That should have made her slam the window shut in a huff, but she leaned even farther out. "Maybe you've got credit."

Knowing full well how foolish it was to argue with a woman when she had her mind made up, Fargo told her that he and his friend might come back by once the place was open for the evening. But they really did need to get somewhere.

"Look, boys, it can be open right now."

Men on the run, Fargo told himself, ought to avoid

controversies. Especially loud disputes in the backyard of the leading bordello in Buckskin Joe. That brassy-voiced gal would surely have hollered on after them if they hadn't started toward the whitewashed back door.

At the door, Sedgwick stood kind of weak-kneed and started to get green around the gills.

"Mister," he muttered, "I ain't never done this afore."

"There's always a first time," Fargo consoled.

"But I ain't sure I knows what to do. An' then some gal will be laughin' at me," he confessed.

"Don't worry none," the Trailsman advised as a mulatto girl let them into the kitchen. "It all comes natural."

They stepped around the table and through the door into the parlor, where the brunette met them. She did have her robe closed. But it didn't matter all that much, the saucy way she sat down on an overstuffed sofa while perching her shapely legs atop an ottoman.

Fargo found himself a chair, leaving one with a better view to young Jim Sedgwick. His goggling eyes were riveted forward, but he did manage to get seated.

The woman looked more than familiar. But before she could explain what name she was working under these days, one of her co-workers sauntered into the room. Naked as a jaybird and quite tall, the new arrival yawned and turned. Her beige pubic thatch confirmed Fargo's suspicion that she looked like a red-head on account of a henna rinse.

"I didn't know we was openin' early today, Polly," she said. "Must be to handle the crowd comin' into town for the hanging tomorrow. Want me to run upstairs and wake up the other girls?"

"No need to, Sadie." Polly shook her brown curls while Sedgwick's eyes got even wider. For some reason, the cowboy seemed to find it tremendously interesting just to watch Sadie breathe.

All this scenery was a pure distraction, one Fargo wanted to let himself enjoy. But something here didn't seem to be sitting right. He figured on asking some questions as soon as it was convenient, and it sure wasn't convenient right now. First things first.

He rose and followed Sadie as she strolled on into the kitchen. "My friend out there," he whispered in her ear, "this is his first time. Think you could do the honors?"

She almost whooped, but caught herself, confining her delight to her smile. "Nothin' I like better than to start a boy right. They don't learn no technique when they mess with the neighbor gal up in some hayloft. An' they never get no manners, neither. This one's on the house."

"Thanks," Fargo said. "I'm sure that when he marries up someday, his wife'll be damn grateful for what he's about to learn from you."

Sadie laughed. "I'll be out as soon as I coffee up so I'm awake enough to work. And I'll get Missy to run up the back stairs and fetch me a gown, too. He'll do better if I start with some clothes on."

Figuring Sadie was a professional who'd know best about such matters, Fargo returned to the parlor. He and Polly indulged in small talk, mostly about how the weather had been so miserable before turning warm again.

She speculated that they would have several weeks of mild, sunny days before the first snowstorm that would stick. And after that, winter would settle in the way it always did. The drifts would pile up in the valleys and savage winds would rake the ridges. Travel would become dangerous and difficult, sometimes impossible. During the winter, the main difference between a mountain town and a prison was that convicts in prison were assured of getting fed regularly.

The Trailsman never got around to offering his own opinion—that a Rocky Mountain winter was best spent in southern Texas—because Sadie arrived from the kitchen. Now rouged up and wearing a slithery floor-length green silk gown that came close to transparency, she sauntered through the parlor. Jim Sedgwick was all eyes. He gulped and stammered some, though, when she took his hand and led the young cowboy past the sofa and up the stairs.

As soon as they heard her door ease shut, Fargo and Polly tiptoed up the stairs to Polly's room. Fargo glanced around; the tiny chamber looked almost luxurious. Flowered wallpaper, shiny brass bedstead, polished oak nightstand with a china pitcher and bowl atop it, Turkish carpet, lace curtains.

"Nice place you've got here," Fargo commented while stepping out of his boots.

"It really ain't," she said as her robe fell to the floor, "but we can talk some later, Skye. Let me help you with that."

Fargo felt quite capable of undressing himself—he'd never had much trouble along that line—but it was one of those things that was a lot more pleasant with a woman's help.

As she stood before the bed, her nimble fingers worked down the row of shirt buttons. She peeled the flannel back and pressed her warm, firm breasts against his muscled belly as she buried her head against his chest. His hands moved round to rub the soft flesh at the small of her back.

Polly held that position for what seemed an eternity to an eager Fargo before lifting her hands. She removed his shirt an arm at a time. Then she lifted her china-doll face. Her green eyes showed evidence of recent tears, although her cupid's-bow mouth bore a smile. But she didn't say anything.

Her arms just moved down his back. Every time her fingers encountered scar tissue, she traced its course, lightly, teasingly. She saw the bandages and was curious; Fargo could see that in those gold-flecked green eyes. He saw something else there, something he couldn't name.

Fargo pulled her tighter, easing his grasp when her hands reached the waistband of his denim trousers, so that there was room between them for her to finesse the buttons of his fly. There'd better be room outside his pants, because there sure wasn't much room left inside.

Polly finished releasing his swelling desire for her. Holding his pulsating shaft in both hands, she sat back on the tatted counterpane that covered the bed. Its springs rustled; she moved her head toward his loins.

The Trailsman's strong hands began to knead her

shoulders as her tongue flicked against the sensitive tip of his organ. The flicks began to merge into a soft, warm continuous progression of tongue-applied pressure. Then her lips pursed around his tip, a circle of pleasure Fargo was more than ready to enjoy.

Polly snapped her head up and rolled back to the bed, her shoulders sliding out from under Fargo's hands. At first he thought she just wanted to get down to some serious screwing, but her frosty expression told him different.

"Okay, Skye Fargo, it's time we talked business." Her voice was steely, and she was crabbing back some, just to be sure she could get to where she'd have an easy lunge for the door, while the bed would block Fargo's way.

"Already told you I don't have any money, honey." Fargo thought he was looking at two different people on the bed. From the neck down, there was a warm, willing woman, displaying more undulating passion than a professional gal generally did.

From the neck up, she was all coldness and logic. "Then we'll trade professional services," she announced, "mine for yours."

Fargo wished his erection would simmer down and quit throbbing so much. Made it hard to think clearly. He knew he'd seen her before, but couldn't come up with anything more specific than that. "As you can see, honey, I'm sure as hell interested in your services. But just what services do you want from me?"

Polly started to grow a grin, the kind a cat displays just after eating a pet canary. "I want out of here."

"Didn't seem to be a damn thing wrong with that door a couple minutes ago," Fargo replied. "Worked just fine. So did the back door."

"That's not what I mean," she fumed, tossing her brown curls. "Out of this town. Today. Before winter sets in. Before Daisy gets back."

Fargo watched her for a few moments before replying. She sat up straighter, her breasts quivering pleasantly. "Thought things looked curious here," he finally said. "It's Daisy Melrose's whorehouse, and Daisy isn't around. Which accounts for the sort of informal way you're operating this afternoon. When's she due back? Or is she ever coming back? Did you gals get a notion to knock off your boss and drop her body down a prospect hole?"

The brown curls should have started standing straight out, judging by the way Polly bristled at the suggestion of murder.

"Damn you, Skye Fargo, you do know who I am. But you've got to believe me. I might have been there, but I wasn't the one that started the fire in St. Louis. I detested Leticia Fidditch, hated that cold bitch with every bone in my body. I didn't burn that awful school, though. But nobody would believe that. Not my best friends. Not even my family."

Still trying to place the woman, Fargo tried to remember fires in distant St. Louis. Sure. About a year ago, a female seminary—the sort of place where rich men sent their daughters to learn how to be elegant ladies, more or less—had burned to the ground. Its proprietor and principal, Miss Leticia Fidditch, was the only casualty, killed by flames and smoke when she ran back inside the building to fetch her Bible.

Just passing through, the Trailsman hadn't paid much mind to the barbershop gossip that one of Miss Fidditch's prize students had set the fire and then left town.

"Well, honey," Fargo consoled, "I do know what it's like to be falsely accused and on the run. You might say that's where I am right now."

She stared at him, wide-eyed. "You mean you and that kid—you're those bank robbers, aren't you? And you've escaped?"

"And you're an arsonist?" Fargo shot back.

"All right," she conceded. "I know who you are, Skye Fargo. You're the Trailsman. One of my school chums pointed you out to me in St. Louis. She said you'd done work for her father, and . . ."

Girls at a prim and proper boarding school had no business sneaking into the parts of St. Louis he frequented. No wonder Polly—her name had doubtless been different at the time—had had such trouble getting along with the Bible-toting, temperance-spouting spinster that ran the place. But Fargo passed mention on that as he leaned forward, his hands finding her shoulders.

"So you lit out West after the fire," he said, his tone as smooth and soothing as the way his hands moved to cup her full breasts. "You changed your name, and you took up the only line of good-paying work most gals can find out here."

Polly's short arms seemed to flutter up toward the big man standing at the edge of her bed. Grasping Fargo's midriff, she tugged him toward her.

"Please, Skye, please," the woman pleaded. "Help me get out of here."

Fargo likely should have asked why leaving would be much of a problem for her, given that Buckskin Joe had regular stage service and a livery stable. But first things first.

Still leaning over her, Fargo pressed her warm torso down. Her back reached the bed moments before his form was atop hers, her legs spreading to surround him. With one straightforward plunge, he was inside her.

"My God," she gasped, "and there's more?"

Fargo thrust deeper in reply.

Forgetting that she was a professional dedicated to getting men in and out as fast as possible, with a minimum of bother, Polly arched upward, determined to engulf as much of this man as she could get.

They settled into a steady but leisurely rhythm of thrust and counterthrust. Whenever Fargo went down, she came up, their loins sliding together to produce shudders of ecstasy on her flushed face. When he retreated, so did she, getting every bit of sensation from each thorough stroke.

"It should always be like this," she murmured, and Fargo couldn't find a reason on earth to disagree with her.

He felt the pressure rising inside him, rising to where there wasn't anything else. No problems in St. Louis for a once-respectable girl to run away from. No mountain walls that might imprison them both. No ramshackle mining camp where people jumped to conclusions, no sheriff that had to notice real soon that his prisoners had escaped, no whorehouse with fancy furniture, no sheets and blankets that smelled of lilac-scented soap. Nothing anywhere but a man and a woman enjoying each other.

With a powerful surge, Fargo released the internal pressure that had blocked out the world. With a most unprofessional giddy shriek, Polly accepted it. Her arms and legs locked around him and clasped tight and tighter, as though she were trying to make sure she didn't miss a bit of him.

Afterward, they caught their breath in the thin air of this town two miles above sea level. Polly's hold on Fargo slackened, but only slightly. She cuddled against him, the warmth welcome as the late afternoon chill settled into the mountains. These Indian summer days could be pleasantly warm, but at night, there was no mistaking the fact that winter would arrive soon.

Muffled noises disturbed Fargo's languor, although Polly didn't seem bothered at all. It must only be household routine, he thought. But when he heard dogs barking outside, he figured it was worth a peek out the window.

Fargo almost wished he hadn't. While the lace curtain brushed against his face, he peered down from his front-facing second-story perch. A two-horse covered carriage, like the kind hacks used in cities, had drawn up, driven by none other than Mayor Tabor.

Without bothering to set the brake—the carriage was at the bottom of a dip and wasn't likely to go anywhere—the eager storekeeper alit. Stocky but stoop-shouldered, he strode quickly to the side door and opened it. Out stepped the bowlegged local sheriff, who in turn lifted his hand to help down a brass-haired woman in a hoopskirt.

She was still a handsome woman. But no matter how much of her ample breasts were displayed by her scooped bodice, no matter how expertly her rouge and powder had been applied, it was more than obvious that her best days were behind her. She had to be Daisy Melrose. While she stood there, twirling a parasol, the postmaster and the lawman began unloading trunks and hatboxes from the rear of the carriage.

Fargo turned and mentioned this arrival to Polly.

"Oh no," she muttered. "The stage must have got in early today."

Wanting to know just what sort of predicament they were both in, Fargo pressed for details. While she explained, he pulled on his clothes, peeking out occasionally. That gave him the minor satisfaction of seeing that the men were still occupied with a small mountain of baggage.

Daisy Melrose was returning from Denver, he learned, where she'd gone on her fall shopping excursion.

Customers at classy whorehouses expected the gals to stay in style, even if the gals really didn't need fashionable clothes, or clothes at all, to do their jobs. Dressmakers were hard to come by in the mountains. So the madame had visited the city to fetch her employees new winter woolens to replace the linens and cottons of summer.

That accounted for her. As for the presence of the two leading citizens of Buckskin Joe, well, Daisy believed in staying on good terms with local authorities.

Fargo peeked out again. "More to it than that," he muttered back. "Old Tabor's stumbled half a dozen times, toting stuff to the front porch, because he's so busy trying to stare down Daisy's dress that he doesn't look where he's stepping."

Polly chuckled. "He does have an eye for the ladies. Poor Mrs. Tabor. She's so kind. Why, she lets us girls shop at her store in daylight, and when the three other respectable women in town complained, she told them to mind their own business."

Fargo couldn't help but laugh to himself. Claiming three respectable women in a mining camp like Buckskin Joe was probably stretching matters. But the important thing now was keeping his neck from getting stretched. He turned again to Polly, who was grudgingly pulling clothes out of the closet and starting to dress.

"Just what is it that keeps you from going downstairs and telling Daisy that you're quitting?"

Polly stepped into a pair of lacy drawers and pulled a chemise over herself before replying. "Miss Daisy believes it's her decision as to when a gal should quit. And if you try to leave before that, you've got trouble."

"Trouble?"

"Can't you see it?" Polly said, the words muffled by the plain cotton shift that covered her face before it settled down on her shoulders. "She's got the local law wrapped up around her little finger, so if they see you out and about, you get brought back here. She's fixed up with the local stage agent, too. When Cock-Eyed Liz tried buying a ticket to Breckenridge, the bastard took her money, then grabbed her and marched her right back here. Livery stable won't rent us horses."

Sensing Fargo's next question, she continued, her voice turning steely again. "And the clothes she gets us—all gaudy and billowy and lacy. You couldn't walk across the street just before sunrise without people spotting you. Not that you could walk very far anyway."

The angry whore held up some high-heeled button shoes that promised very unsteady footing. "Walk in these? The ground's rough around here. You'd fall down all the time. Besides that, Miss Daisy always gets us shoes that are a little on the small side. They pinch and your feet hurt awfully about two minutes after you put these shoes on."

Glancing out the window again, Fargo saw that the men had one more trip to make before everything would be inside—no doubt them included. He could jump off the second story and take off running, but he doubted that Polly could manage it. Going through the downstairs would almost certainly mean a fight, and the sheriff packed a gun.

There were other considerations, too, such as young Jim Sedgwick down the hall. Fargo felt his internal edginess rise, then told it to back down, so that he could take a slow and leisurely look around the room. A madam that didn't trust her girls with shoes sure as hell wouldn't let them keep derringers. But there had to be something here he could use.

He spied a small, ornate hand-held mirror atop her dresser. Its silver-plated handle forked into two prongs, perhaps six inches apart. The mirror swiveled between the prongs. Next to it lay a simple necklace. In dim light, it might have fooled somebody into thinking that there were real pearls on the string.

"Polly," Fargo hissed, "you gals must use something to keep your silk stockings from falling down when you wear 'em."

She looked perplexed. "You mean garters?" she finally answered.

Exasperated, Fargo grunted agreement. "Bring me one."

Moments later, they were standing at the dresser as she handed him a band of rubber an inch wide and three or four inches long when it was lying flat. "Go down the hall and fetch Sedgwick," he muttered, "fast. Real fast. I don't care what he's doin'. Get him here."

Her silent but swift departure prevented any argument about what he was fixing to do with her fancy mirror and string of fake pearls. Grinning in spite of the situation, Fargo grabbed the prongs that held the mirror in place and pulled them apart like a wishbone.

The glass came out, leaving the Y-shaped framework. He popped one end of the necklace in his mouth and bit hard with his front teeth, his incisors sliding back and forth until the internal string was cut. He slid the beads into his pocket. The garter took a little stretching to fit over the prongs on the mirror frame.

Edging back to the window, Fargo saw the mayor and the sheriff standing next to the carriage. One big trunk remained, and they didn't seem to be in any hurry about picking it up. But while their backs were to him, Fargo eased the window open.

Grinning like a boy full of mischief, the Trailsman recalled that the last time he'd used a slingshot, he hadn't even started shaving. They were a kid's toy to be given up when a fellow learned how to use a rifle.

The two men outside were now wrestling with the heavy trunk. In the baggage area behind the carriage cab, the sheriff crouched, trying to transfer some of the trunk's weight to the grunting Tabor, whose feet were on the ground. Even so, he didn't look any steadier that his companion.

Fargo took aim and let loose with a bead.

More than twenty years had passed since the last time he'd tried to hit anything that way. So Fargo had an excuse for shooting long the first time and short the second. Neither man down there seemed to notice, which stood to reason. Who'd hear a fake pearl hitting the ground when there was a stamp mill running nearby? Judging by the way they were both weaving and staggering, the trunk was all they could pay much mind to, anyway.

Fargo's third shot came closer, striking the near carriage horse on its butt. From that distance with such a puny force, the dappled gelding would have been more perturbed by a fly bite. Even so, the critter visibly tensed.

Feeling more competent with his new weapon, Fargo nailed the far horse in about the same spot, with about the same result. His first and second tries for belly shots went low, sailing just under the horses to plunk into the gravel that flanked the road.

But the next shot whizzed into the near horse, at a tender spot low on its belly. The critter didn't like that at all. Stung, it looked up, ears erect, nostrils flaring, teeth bared. Something was annoying hell out of the horse, and the horse couldn't reach to swish it with his bobbed tail.

When it got bit again in the same spot, the horse took serious offense at this new nuisance. The gelding snorted and reared forward, rocking the carriage with a sudden jolt.

Lurching backward and unable to keep his feet under him, the sheriff tumbled, which sent the full weight of the trunk onto Tabor. He staggered for a moment, then collapsed onto the rocky surface of the road. The man didn't seem to know two things: heads weren't built for driving stones into the earth, and chests weren't made for catching heavy trunks. Considering how still his body got, the storekeeper likely didn't know much of anything at the moment. He was out cold.

His companion fared better, more or less. Landing

in a face-first sprawl right atop the trunk, the sheriff rolled off. Shaking himself, he got up just in time to see the carriage bounce away, headed for whatever might be at the end of the road. Indecision showing on his pained face, he glanced at his inert companion, then took off running after the carriage.

The room door flew open. Fargo spun, loaded sling-shot in his hands. Jim Sedgwick looked mighty upset about having his lessons interrupted. Polly, though, looked even testier about what had happened to her mirror and necklace. Giving neither of them time to complain, the Trailsman sprang across the bed.

"Let's go," he urged. "Where's the back stairs?"

With no more noise than a herd of buffalo might make, they arrived moments later in the kitchen. The back door stood tantalizingly close. To get to it, though, they'd have to argue with Miss Daisy. Or to be more precise, the double-barreled sawed-off scattergun Miss Daisy was holding.

4

There were certain things that no man with a lick of sense ever did: draw to an inside straight; get between a grizzly sow and her cubs; and argue with a woman holding a loaded shotgun—especially one standing only a couple paces in front of you.

"Going somewhere?" Miss Daisy asked. She tightened her grip on the greener to where Fargo could see her knuckles whiten. Most employers didn't seem to take it quite that seriously when one of their employees wanted to leave. For all that, most business owners did get riled when somebody didn't pay—but not this riled.

Removing his stare from Miss Daisy's hard-set face, Fargo flicked his eyes to his companions. Bunched at the bottom of the stairs, they were frozen in front of him. He couldn't see their faces. He had to guess by how they stood.

Right below his eyes, Polly quivered like an aspen leaf in a summer storm. The hairs on the back of her neck bristled atop goosebumps; her flesh was pale. She gulped for her air in shallow gasps. Right next to her, young Jim Sedgwick was breathing easy, although he was flushed beneath his tan. He was in condition to act. But there wasn't any way to tell him what to do.

Imperceptibly moving his eyes back to Miss Daisy and her shotgun, Fargo knew the woman would be out of action for a minute or two after she fired it. The recoil would slam her back, stunning her as it bruised her shoulder. Trouble was, double-ought buckshot at this close range would very likely put him and his companions out of action for good.

All Fargo had to counter the buckshot were a couple dozen fake pearls. Keeping his eyes on Miss Daisy and his shoulders rigid, he slid his hand down and pulled several beads from his pocket. Only then did he bother to answer her question, breaking an eternity of silence.

"Fact is, Miss Daisy, we were fixing to go somewhere."

Miss Daisy's grip grew tighter.

"Polly better change her plans. She's not going anywhere." Her glacial eyes, narrowed to brilliant points, focused momentarily on Sedgwick and lingered on Fargo. "You two bank robbers are going back to jail, so they can hang you tomorrow."

Sedgwick's voice was still reedy, but it wasn't quivering. "What makes you so sure we're them?"

"They just found out about it when my stage pulled in. It's all over town what you did to poor old Pete Green. Too bad they can't hang you twice. Sheriff Bogardus will be here any minute."

Fargo knew better, but didn't see any reason to enlighten the gun-wielding madam. Not as long as her eyes were fixed on Sedgwick, anyway. Keeping his hand low, he maneuvered a bead atop his thumbnail. Recalling another childhood skill, he hooked his thumb under his forefinger and flicked the fake pearl.

It shot up from behind Polly's trembling back, just clearing her shoulder. Fargo couldn't have asked for a better trajectory. The tiny sphere arced over Miss Daisy, then struck a tinware pitcher on a shelf behind her. In the silence which gripped the room, the trifling plunk sounded like a cannon to Miss Daisy.

Her hardened face snapped upward, turning toward the source of the sound. The gun rose as her head turned.

Now given the choice between a certain hanging and a possible shooting, Sedgwick dived forward. His narrow shoulders drove into Miss Daisy's hoopskirt at knee level, toppling the woman back.

Jumping off his left leg, the Trailsman sprang into Sedgwick's former spot. Landing on his right and springing forward, he flew ahead, his arms extended, hands ready to grab the short but deadly shotgun.

Sprawled on her back and no doubt surprised, the madam had grabbed the stock with one hand and the barrel with the other. Holding the gun like a rolling pin, she was swinging it up and over. The idea was to cave in Sedgwick's head, planted somewhere by her knees.

The cowboy was trying to move upward, but the ruffled hoopskirt was in his way. Miss Daisy wriggled like a fresh-caught trout, except trout don't kick. And her pointed shoes were thrashing in Sedgwick's crotch. Holding on was about the best any man might do in that situation.

Fargo's airborne lunge knocked the gun out of Miss Daisy's hands. He grasped, but the weapon fell back. When he landed on his knees right over Miss Daisy's head, he reached again for the gun.

The gun didn't seem quite so important an instant later, though. A staggering spasm of intense pain shot up his thigh. Miss Daisy's teeth, having gained a fair-sized bite, began to twist the chunk of bleeding flesh they gripped.

Bringing both fists down on her head made a lot of sense, but Fargo couldn't bring himself to do that to a woman. Even this woman. He yanked her hair, forcing her mouth open. As soon as his thigh was free of her teeth, he swung to the side.

She didn't waste any time either. Her right hand, now free to swing up, carried five long, sharp fingernails. They raked Fargo's face, drawing blood. His eyelids clamped shut by reflex, Fargo didn't see her follow-up assault.

But he sure felt it. Her thumb was probing for an eye socket, so she could dig in a nail and gouge out half of his vision.

Savagely, Fargo grabbed the woman's arm and twisted. With relief, he felt the vicious, penetrating fingernails lift from his face. Fargo slowly opened his eyes, in time to see Miss Daisy going for another bite. But next to her head, there were bare feet. Moments later, the butt of the shotgun slammed into Miss Daisy's blond curls.

Fargo looked up the gun to see Polly's hands on the

barrels. She stared down at him, wide-eyed. "I didn't kill her, did I?" she finally asked.

"Reckon not," Fargo replied. His face stung and getting up was downright agonizing, thanks to the way Miss Daisy had chomped his thigh. Even so, he could stand straighter than Sedgwick. Hunched up and using the back wall for support, the cowboy had trouble catching his breath.

Just to avoid any further complications with women and shotguns, Fargo eased the greener out of Polly's trembling hands. She didn't seem to notice. "Let's get out of here," she pleaded. "I want to go."

"No argument there," Fargo agreed. But it was best to look before one leaped. Gingerly opening the back door, Fargo looked out. Although the sky was still bright and blue, the yard and lower slopes beyond were enveloped in long shadows cast by the enormous peaks that rimmed Buckskin Joe.

Fargo would have preferred something more substantial for cover, but the semidarkness would have to do. They bolted to the woodshed. From there, they had a winding alley lined with other woodsheds, as well as privies and stables. Like a prairie cottontail scatting from sagebrush to sagebrush, hoping that no hawks were watching, they scatted toward the center of town.

They crept inside one of the more substantial woodsheds. Its whipsawed planks were thick enough to stop most rifle rounds, so anybody coming after them would have to come close—close enough for the shotgun to be effective.

While Sedgwick stood guard by leaning on a pile of stove-length splits and peering out a knothole, Polly apologized for waiting so long to club her former boss.

"Well, sooner would have been better," Fargo replied, "but I was damn glad you came along when you did." He rubbed the deep scratches on his face and wondered how long it would be before he could take a straight step without feeling a torrent of agony from his thigh. "That gal sure could put up a fight."

"It's something you learn real fast in our trade," Polly whispered back. "When you're in bed with nothing on, and a man turns surly on you, you've got to defend yourself."

Fargo nodded. "Stands to reason." Realizing there was no need to stand so tense and ready, he induced a big yawn and stretched. At least his arms moved freely. "Soon as it gets good and dark, we'll be on our way."

"Maybe not," Sedgwick hissed. "Somebody's comin'."

Polly sidled back into the dark corner farthest from the door. Fargo got next to the door, shotgun at ready. Sedgwick just stayed put, no more perturbed than a setting hen atop her eggs.

The Trailsman found out why when the door opened. They had to have taken shelter in the woodshed behind Buckskin Joe's general store and post office, because it was Augusta Tabor who stepped in for a fresh load of fuel. His eyes fully adjusted to the dim and fading light, Fargo could see that she held two canvas contraptions for toting wood, so she could get more than an armload back to the store.

She got flustered and dropped them noiselessly to the chip-laden dirt floor when Fargo turned and said "Good evenin', Mrs. Tabor."

Augusta recovered quickly, although her hands kept twisting and pulling on her apron. "I might have known," she finally said. "Isn't there any place else you could have hidden?"

"Just happened this way," Fargo assured her. "Not many woodsheds big enough for all three of us. Stables are stinkful, and privies are even worse."

The diminutive woman started to laugh, but caught herself. "Three of you? There were only two."

Their female companion shuffled toward Augusta. "You know me, Mrs. Tabor. I'm Polly Warner."

Augusta didn't shake hands, because she seemed put out. Not at Polly Warner, precisely. "Then maybe you can tell me what happened up there at Miss Daisy's. My Horace just came home staggering, except he hadn't been drinking. I heard there was a commotion up at your, er, house of ill repute, but of course Horace doesn't know anything about it. He always denies that he goes anywhere near that place, but I know better."

"He was just trying to be helpful, unloading some stuff from a carriage, when the horses bolted and a trunk landed on him," Fargo volunteered. "I can't say what your husband might or might not do there other times, Mrs. Tabor, but that's God's truth about how he got the wind knocked out of himself this afternoon. I saw it myself."

"Well, he shouldn't have been anywhere near that nest of trollops in the first place," Augusta snapped. She paused and breathed deep a couple times. When her conversation resumed, she sounded friendlier. "I'm sorry," she said. "That's not your concern."

Sedgwick broke the silence. "Mrs. Tabor, what's the talk in town right now? Who all's after us?"

"They're considering those matters at this moment," she replied. "The menfolk are holding a town meeting in the store, trying to get up a posse and track you down."

"All of them?" Fargo asked.

"All of them that worry about such things," Mrs. Tabor replied. "Now, if you'll excuse me, I'd best take some wood to the stove."

For the first time, Fargo noticed that the shed was chilly. "Much obliged, Mrs. Tabor. Need any help with the wood?"

"No thank you. Keeping that place clean is enough bother. If they caught sight of you . . ."

Fargo and Sedgwick did stack firewood on the canvas slings while Polly sidled over to her and asked about some shoes. Augusta was thoughtful for a moment, then said that some Utes had ridden through a couple weeks ago. Willing to trade most anything for sugar, they'd left several pair of elkskin moccasins. "Just come on up to the back door with me," she said as she grasped a sling handle with each hand.

As soon as Polly returned and got herself shod, lacing the calf-length leggings with rawhide thongs, they lit out of the woodshed. For several hundred yards, they stayed together, walking slowly down the alley.

Not knowing his way around town all that well, Fargo gazed intently toward the street every time there was a break between structures. He finally spotted the

55

shadowy outline of the jail building and knew they were behind the sheriff's office.

"I'm going to go fetch my Colt," he advised. "You head on up to the livery stable and figure out our possibles and horses and the like."

"Where do we meet?" Sedgwick whispered.

"Corral gate," Fargo answered. "Unless a ruckus starts. Then you two light out any way you can. I'll manage."

As they went on up the alley, Fargo sidled around the sheriff's office. Generally, there was a jail in back of such facilities, but for whatever reasons, folks in Buckskin Joe put their prisoners across the street. The log building had but two rooms. The back one was dark, but a coal-oil lamp glowed in the front room.

Fargo ducked under the window as he went by, so he didn't get a long look at the room. His quick glance revealed that the lamp sat on a table, next to a straight-backed chair. Just in case anybody might try to sneak in there and steal the chair, Pete Green was sitting on it. Seeing that the street was empty, save for a few folks staggering into and out of saloons, Fargo went on around and swung the front door open.

Green looked up. Fargo planned to tell the old shit to go fetch his gunbelt from the side wall, where it hung on a peg. Then maybe he'd throw the jailer back into his own jail.

But Pete Green had been in the wrong line the day they were handing out brains, or even common sense. As he saw Fargo, a wave of disbelief and shock crossed his lined, wizened face. As the man rose from his chair, his right hand dropped to the old Remington cap-and-ball revolver on his hip.

Although he didn't mind killing Pete Green, Fargo did hate the noise the shotgun made. A dozen chunks of double-ought buckshot—each the size of a bullet from a small pistol—roared across the room. Four of them caught the jailer's still-hunched body, ripping a hat-sized hole in his midsection.

Gore splatted against the back wall. Moments later, Green's lifeless carcass rolled back, toppling the chair as he thudded to the floor. For a moment, his skinny legs twitched.

Most of the other buckshot had harmlessly peppered the table and wall. But one had caught the base of the lamp, shattering it and spraying coal oil. In moments, the flame had spread from the wick to a spreading pool of orange fire. Fargo leaped through the sooty but sweet-smelling black smoke to grab his Colt.

Spinning around to get out, he saw the flames had spread with surprising speed. A pool of fire licked at his feet. He sprang forward to the nearest spot where there wasn't fire.

The thick smoke obscured Green's body and the chair in that spot. Fargo stumbled as his toes stubbed into the corpse and the chair barked his shins. It was a struggle to keep his feet under him so he wouldn't pitch forward into the growing blaze. By spinning on the balls of his feet, he managed. But the effort cost him time, time enough for the flames to surround him by the time he again stood straight.

Thick and choking smoke swirled up from the hellish floor. The cloud stung his eyes. Fargo couldn't help but blink furiously. Not that it would have done much good to keep his eyes open. All there was to see was fire and smoke. He had nothing besides his instincts to tell him where the door or window might be. Those might not be reliable, the way he'd had to spin around when he'd landed here.

His ears told him that the fire was getting serious. Coal oil burned with a quiet hiss, now joined by the spitting and crackling of blazing wood. Maddened, Fargo kicked Green's body forward into the flames, flames that leaped as high as his shoulders.

The Trailsman didn't have time for any twinges of conscience about using a man's body for a stepping-stone. When he forced his eyes to blink open, he saw the sprawled form as a dark spot. Its outstretched arm reached into another shadowy area where the flames had not yet spread.

Fargo leaped, left leg bounding forward. Green almost tripped him again. Fargo's boot landed on what was left of the man's midriff, a slippery mess where the buckshot had torn him open. Momentum propelled them both toward the edge of the flames as Fargo kicked at the flaming floor with his right foot. The heat was overpowering. The stench of burning hair joined the nauseating stink of the dense smoke.

All that Fargo could see at first was a wall. Make that two walls, a corner. He recalled the story about Miss Fidditch in St. Louis. A familiar Colt might be generally more useful than a Bible. But staying around a fire to grab one's gun was starting to look just about as stupid, and as deadly, as running back into a burning building to fetch the Good Book. Fargo figured he'd keep that in mind next time. If there was a next time.

Shutting his eyes to the smoke, trying to make sure he breathed through his nose no matter how bad the smoke stank, Fargo felt his way along the wall, away from the corner. He knew better, but he could have sworn that blisters were sprouting on his hands.

Never mind. He finally felt the edge of the window. Gritting his teeth as he grasped the scorching barrel of his Colt, he clubbed out three or four panes. The sound of shattering glass was overpowered by the roar of the flames at his back.

Hoping he'd made himself a hole that wouldn't cut his body to ribbons, Fargo twisted and went through shoulder first. He landed outdoors in a heap. Grateful to feel the rush of cold, fresh night air, he held his position, breathed deep, and listened.

There was more bustle in the street than before, he was sure. But a fire that was blazing like this one should have drawn as many folks as a hanging. Besides that, they'd be trying to put out the fire with a bucket brigade or a pump cart or whatever they had. Generally that did about as much good as pissing on the fire. About all they could do was try to prevent the blaze from spreading, which meant hauling gunpowder charges into the adjacent buildings and blowing them up. Meanwhile, everyone would be hoping that no wind-borne embers landed on distant roofs.

After clambering to his feet, Fargo stepped into the

shadows, away from the glare that poured out of the window. There he realized that he was between walls. The flames hadn't yet reached the roof of the sheriff's office, which would have caused a general alarm. And if any folks had walked by and noticed anything unusual about how bright it appeared inside, they hadn't been sober enough to care.

Fargo didn't feel any fresh cuts from his dive through the window. But he did feel some obligation to keep Buckskin Joe from turning into cinders before morning. There were some good folks here, even if they didn't exactly run things.

Gaining confidence that nothing important on his body had been injured, he moved toward the street. Fargo got there just as a bunch of four burly but frolicsome miners were staggering out of the Deadfall Saloon, thirty or forty yards away.

Fargo hollered to get their attention. They were so busy slapping each other on the back and talking about how great it would be to crawl into bed with Silver Heels that they paid him no heed. He shouted "Fire!" and he might as well have whispered "Ignore me" for all the good it did.

Finally he shot his Colt at the brightest star in the sky. The star just kept on twinkling, but the miners froze in their tracks and turned his way. "Goddamn it," Fargo bellowed, "there's a fire." He pointed at the sheriff's office.

They didn't seem to know what to do about it except to approach him. "Get on up to Tabor's store," the Trailsman hollered. "Fetch some help there." The quartet of miners took off like scalded cats, headed one way. Moving even faster, Fargo ran the other way, toward the livery stable.

There wasn't much light, but Fargo liked what he saw at the corral gate, back behind the stable. Astride their mounts, Jim Sedgwick and Polly Warner sat there waiting calmly. Between their horses, the saddled Ovaro stood ready; they'd even remembered to shove Fargo's Sharps carbine into its saddle boot.

By now, flames were leaping out the front door of the sheriff's office.

"Jesus, Fargo," Sedgwick muttered. "Did you have to go to all that trouble just to get your gun?"

Swinging into the saddle, Fargo nudged his big pinto into motion before answering. "The fire wasn't really my notion," he explained as crowd noises drifted in from behind them. "All I wanted was my Colt, but the late Pete Green just had to get quarrelsome on me."

A puff of sick-smelling smoke passed them at that moment. It made Fargo remember the image of Green's gut-shot body, sprawled in the flames. He changed the subject. "Have any trouble getting the horses?"

"Not really," Sedgwick answered. Polly rode silently and the horses slowed, because they were climbing a steep, rocky grade in the dark. "Polly here just went in the front door and I went around to the back. Found our saddles and tack and possibles jammed into a stall, so I sorted 'em out and went out to the corral. Wasn't too much work to get us saddled up, even in the dark. 'Cept for that Ovaro of yours. He don't cotton much to strangers. But we made friends, I reckon."

Sedgwick stopped talking long enough to look back. The local fire company was in action. They had run a hose down to the creek. In the middle of the street, the hose led to a pump on wheels. Its central rod rocked like a seesaw as four men, two on each end, worked it up and down. The pressurized water went into a short hose. Two men maneuvered its nozzle, directing water at the flames now sprouting from the roof.

Others scurried about, in and out of adjacent buildings, probably planting explosives inside. The flickering flames showed folks on nearby rooftops, swatting embers and sparks with wet gunnysacks. The night air was still, so they had at least a fair chance of saving their town.

To keep from thinking about it, Fargo asked Polly what had happened in the front of the livery while Sedgwick fetched the gear and horses.

For a few moments, Fargo thought she hadn't heard him, or didn't want to answer, because she was still staring at the flame-lit activity back in Buckskin Joe.

He didn't blame her, really; it was quite a show. But it was something he didn't want to think about. He didn't know any way to change what had happened, and he didn't see how he could have done anything differently. Sometimes things just turned out that way, and the best you could ask was to come out alive. Those flames had come mighty close.

Eventually, she answered, her voice giddy. "I just walked in and told the night man that I wanted to rent a buggy. He's a once-a-month regular, every payday, so he knew me and said he wasn't supposed to rent to any of Miss Daisy's soiled doves."

"Not very fair of him," Fargo prodded. "He got to rent pretty much whatever he wanted from you."

"I mentioned that," she continued. "I even said we might be able to work out some sort of deal up in the hayloft, and all the time, I leaned low against the counter, just to make sure he had a good view of what he might expect. At first, he was pretty steadfast. We talked for quite a spell. Maybe he would have come around, but then Jim here came up behind him and hit him upside the head with his pistol butt. Then we just waited for you."

She turned again to look back at the fire, as did Jim Sedgwick. Fargo couldn't resist joining them. The blaze had dimmed considerably, and it wasn't just because they were now more distant.

Mostly they saw orange smoke and glowing, log-sized coals, although sporadic tongues of flame licked upward. The stream of water still sprayed on the fire, so likely it was under control unless the wind sprang up. Looking upward, Fargo saw no clouds, and there hadn't been a breeze worth mention all evening. Like big puffballs, the smoke and steam hovered over the ruins of the sheriff's office. The Trailsman felt relieved that he hadn't started a whole town on fire.

"Don't reckon they'll manage to get up a posse for a while," Sedgwick commented.

"So that's why you started the fire," Polly added.

Every time Fargo inhaled, the acrid stench of singed hair assaulted his nose. He brushed at his beard, but the odor lingered. "You're a gal that likes to make deals," he told Polly, "so I've got an offer I surely hope you'll take me up on."

"Let's hear it."

"I won't ask you about your fire, and you don't ask me about mine." Lest Sedgwick feel left out, he directed the rest of his remarks to the cowboy. "The only fire I want to think about for the rest of the night is a campfire. You got any notions about where we might set up?"

"Mayhaps. Lemme study on it some. Gotta figure out where we are, first."

They rode through an engulfing blackness relieved only by the stars overhead and the waning glow from Buckskin Joe, burning behind them.

5

Their route climbed steadily, parallel to the splashing creek. For the first mile or so, they followed a wagon road. From the meticulous way the horses stepped, taking their time as though they were going up an eternal flight of stairs, they had passed the limit for wheels. This was a steep and winding pack trail to the highest mines, diggings that pecked at the crest of the Mosquito Range.

The horses sped up a little and quit breathing so hard as they crossed a reasonably level stretch. When the grade again began to climb, Sedgwick reined up and dismounted.

Fargo met him on the ground. "Need to let your critter blow?" he asked.

"Wouldn't hurt," the cowboy replied as he fiddled with some stuff tied behind his saddle. "But I was startin' to shiver, an' Polly's wearin' less'n I am." He found a coat and passed it up to the grateful woman.

Fargo admired her for not complaining, even though she had to have been close to miserable in this still, frosty air. He wished, though, that she'd mentioned it earlier. Then he knew he should have realized she'd need more than that cotton shift. After the narrow escape from the sheriff's fiery office, this cold air felt so good to Fargo that he'd forgotten that his companions might not feel the same way.

Turning, he noticed that the heavy coat was winning its wrestling match with Polly. She struggled to get it around her while staying mounted. Since the stirrups hung considerably below her feet, her task was complicated. Fargo extended an arm and helped her down.

"Thank you," she stammered, trying to keep anyone from guessing that she was shivering. Sedgwick materialized at her other side. In moments, the woman was clad in wool from her shoulders to her ankles.

"You're welcome," the men answered in unison.

"This a fit spot to camp?" Fargo asked Sedgwick. "You know this country better than I do, 'specially at night."

"I misdoubt that," the cowboy answered. "When we trailed beef between our ranch an' Buckskin, we always swung through to the south, over Weston Pass. Asides, we always saw fit to bed down long afore it got this dark outside."

Fargo probed his memory. "We've been riding up Buckskin Creek. We've kept going up, so we've not crossed any ridge big enough to matter. So we can't be too far from Kite Lake at the head of the creek."

"Shee-it," Sedgwick said. "I figgered the same, but I was sure hopin' you'd say different."

"Why? What's wrong with a lake?" Polly interjected.

While he studied on their options, Fargo let Sedgwick explain.

For somebody on horseback, Kite Lake was a dead end. Except for the way they would come in, the small pool was surrounded by tremendous walls more than a thousand feet high. The middle was a solid cliff, one face of towering Mount Lincoln. That cliff tapered off both ways into vast and steep slopes of scree—millions of treacherous, jagged rocks. For every upward step, you'd slide back two.

"You and your kin rode in over Mosquito Pass, didn't you?" Fargo asked, interrupting Sedgwick's explanation that Kite Lake was named for its shape.

"That we did," he answered. "From Oro up to the top, then down to Alma, where this gulch strikes that one, an' back up to Buckskin." After a thoughtful pause, the cowboy continued. "Say, Fargo, why didn't we light out down that way, 'stead of goin' up?"

Polly answered, which was just as well, since Fargo felt exasperated by such a question. "Wouldn't the posse expect us to go that way?"

"Go to the head of the class," Fargo said. "Besides that, the country gets gentler that way. Folks can follow you across grass and dirt. Up here in the rocks, tracking gets tedious as hell."

Sedgwick took his time before speaking. "Guess I should've consulted you afore I took up robbin' banks. One way or t'other, they'd've got us. Me an' my brother Red an' our cousins." When he mentioned his family, his thin voice broke on the words.

For several minutes he tried, with limited success, to keep his sobs inaudible. Then he broke down. "I'm sorry, Mr. Fargo. Can't help it. They was all the family I had. An' then today, bustin' outta jail, an' the fight with Miss Daisy . . ."

"Seems to me something else happened to you today, too," Fargo consoled.

Some strength returned to Sedgwick's voice. "How the hell could I disremember that?" he marveled. "Sadie. We done it three times. Shee-it. I done become a man today." His voice got firmer. "Better start actin' like one."

They remounted, Sedgwick in the lead as they angled toward the creek, then crossed the yard-wide freshet, trusting their horses to find good footing. They weren't making time worth mention. Without anyone actually saying so, they agreed that staying in motion made sense as a way to stay warm, seeing as they were above timberline, where firewood was mighty scarce.

Perhaps a quarter mile past the creek crossing, Sedgwick dismounted. "As best I know, it's just a steep, long walk from here up to the ridge that divides Buckskin Gulch from Mosquito Gulch. Last time I looked up at it, didn't appear all that sharp. So we oughtta be able to follow it west some, work our way to the saddle, an' drop on down the other side of Mosquito Pass to Oro."

Fargo had figured out the same thing. But he knew the trip would work better if this exhausting, treacherous route was Sedgwick's idea. Polly said that as long as they'd stop whenever she got winded, she was willing to try.

Leading the Ovaro, with Polly's mount tethered behind, Fargo picked his way up the slope. Polly had wanted to go last, but he made her walk ahead.

"I'll just slow you down," she protested. "You go on up, and maybe I'll catch up."

There were only about a thousand things that could go wrong for folks scrambling around on rocks in the darkness, and Fargo was trying to minimize those risks. "No," he told her, "we stay close together. We take it real slow. Fact is, I want you to keep talking, chattering, singing, whatever, the whole time."

"But why? I have enough trouble breathing, let alone talking or singing."

"Because if you can't talk while you're climbing, you're climbing too fast. You'll get winded. You'll have to sit down to catch your breath. Then your muscles will tighten up on you. Just go slow and steady without stopping. Doesn't matter how slow, as long as it's steady. And don't worry about getting lost. As long as we're going uphill, we're going the right way."

It was too much to hope that Sedgwick, who started up the slope with long, hurried strides, would pay any heed to Fargo's advice. A man could take those steps here, even in the dark. Although the climb was rocky and steep, this hillside wasn't quite as steep as the others. Its rocks sat more comfortably; they didn't bound for the valley floor with the slightest disturbance. In spots where dust had managed to settle and become soil, thatches of grass sprouted, a welcome relief for feet that got assaulted by the rocks, whose sharp edges could be felt even through heavy boot soles.

Still, going up it meant climbing into the sky at a fearsome gradient that could knock the wind out of anyone who got in a hurry. Sedgwick would figure that out, sooner or later.

Polly didn't think she knew better, so she took Fargo's advice. Not more than a couple steps ahead, she kept up a constant chatter, punctuated with deep breaths every second or third step. Most of it was mindless gossip. Nobody thought all that clearly in this thin air. After an hour or so, she ran out of ideas and started spouting nursery rhymes.

"With silver bells and cockleshells, and pretty maids all in a row." After answering the old question about contrary Mistress Mary's garden, Fargo joined her for the chorus of "Old King Cole." Glad that nobody was around to hear how foolish they must sound, he helped with a few more ditties.

Their pace was so slow that Fargo felt neither tired nor winded. But his head felt so light that it might just float away. "You lost considerable blood in that bank shoot-up," he muttered to himself. "Takes a while to get it all back."

Polly's latest childish question drifted in. With effort, Fargo shifted his attention and replied, "Sugar and spice and all that's nice."

"And what are little boys . . . Oh dear." Deep gasps replaced the brushing of moccasin on granite. "This little boy," she said, pausing between each word, "he's not snips or puppy dog tails. He's all snail."

Fargo moved up to her. Only six paces, but he gained his own height in that distance.

Overhead, the stars shone as brightly as stars ever do, brilliant glints shimmering in the clear mountain sky. Such light as they provided gave shape to the rock-strewn slope. Not enough light, though, to show any details.

Polly had stubbed her toe against a shape that could be distinguished from the rest of the hillside only by its relative smoothness.

Fargo knelt and waited until he could hear something besides the whoosh of air rushing in and out his own lungs. Here, his sensitive ears had to tell him the situation.

First to emerge as a distinct sound was the slow respiration of the horses. Two behind him. Sedgwick's, over to the right, downhill several lengths. Annoyed by where it was standing, since its steel shoes occasionally ground against the granite.

Then Polly's breaths, like the rustle of leaves. Finally, Sedgwick. Slow and easy, but with some disconcerting wheezes and rattles. The cowboy lay halfway curled up, so that Polly had bumped into his shins. Crabbing delicately, to keep from dislodging rocks onto the prone man, Fargo worked up to the boy's head.

His rib cage was rising and falling regular enough. Likely he'd just gotten tuckered out from going too fast, had stopped to rest, and had then fallen asleep.

Time to wake the knothead and get him moving again, at a more sensible clip. Squatting from the rocks, Fargo reached over for the boy's shoulder. Something didn't look right. A blotch where there should have been a mouth and chin.

The blotch was sticky. Blood.

"Polly?"

"What, Skye?" She inhaled sharply. "Is he all right?"

"He's alive."

"What's that mean?"

"I don't know. There's blood all over his face."

Her moccasins brushed against the rocks as she came around from the downhill side. Her coat hem snagged on Sedgwick's hat as she knelt. Her tiny hands joined Fargo's to explore the blood as Sedgwick lay there, unperturbed.

"Maybe it's just a nosebleed," she whispered. "The altitude sometimes does that to newcomers."

The thought was cheering, but unlikely. "He's lived in the high country for a couple years."

"I didn't hear him coughing, though."

"Would you have? Over our talking? And your own breathing?" Fargo hated to dismay her. But there was no sense getting your hopes up without good reason. And Sedgwick had so far given them little cause for optimism.

"Probably not." She shuddered and pressed her shoulder against Fargo's side.

"Damn if I know what to do."

"Can't you just wake him up? And if he's not able to walk, couldn't one of the horses carry him?"

Just being led, the horses had enough trouble picking their way upward. Putting a load on was asking for a broken leg. But there was more to it than that.

"I'm no doctor, Polly. So I don't rightly know what the exact problem is, but I've seen it happen. When men get up this high and start moving too fast, they gulp down every breath. Then something pops loose in their lungs, and next thing you know, they're coughing blood out the mouth. Then they collapse. Moving them just makes it worse. Not that there's much you can do for them, anyway."

Polly's slow nod rubbed against his shoulder. "Just last month I saw it happen. To a gent I was in bed with. They called the doctor."

She leaned forward and placed her ear against Sedgwick's flank, and held it there for better than a minute.

"If that old quack wasn't lying, then I think Jim's going to come around."

"Why's that?" Fargo asked as he stood and stretched, trying to shake out some of the cramps that had invaded his thighs.

"Well, the doctor used a something-scope to listen to my bleeding gent's chest. He let me listen too—after he fondled me considerable by listening to my heart. Anyway, he said that if you didn't hear any gurgling sounds, then nothing major had been broken. I heard some rasps and wheezes and rattles in this boy. But nothing that sounds like the gushing and bubbling we heard in my late customer."

She waited for Fargo to tell her that she shouldn't be so sanguine about Sedgwick's prospects. But instead, he just stretched his arm down and helped her stand up. "Hope you're right," he finally said.

6

Snails. Turtles. Glaciers. Molasses in January. A saloon moocher reaching for his pocket when it's his turn to buy a round.

Fargo knew this trip would fit in there somewhere. Set one foot right in front of the other. Transfer your weight to the upper leg. Suck in a breath. Next foot. Exhale.

This was about as exciting as watching grass grow, but there wasn't any other way to get Jim Sedgwick up to the ridge, once they'd roused him.

At first, the cowboy had coughed and sputtered something awful. Fargo and Polly had to brace him when he took his first steps. Even with that help, he stood spindly-legged, like a newborn colt. He was so addle-headed that he couldn't even cuss straight.

But the cowboy was moving. Footstep after plodding footstep, the procession inched up the slope. Polly Warner was in the lead, on her third or fourth go-round with the nursery rhymes as she set the tedious pace. Jim Sedgwick struggled in the middle, using every iota of concentration he could muster, just to put his feet in the right places. The Trailsman walked drag, leading the string of three ambling horses.

Eventually, the grade eased. About that time, a ragged rim of pink emerged to the east. The dimmer stars imperceptibly faded into the graying sky.

Grateful that there was now some scenery to break the monotony, Fargo took his bearings. The dark line pressed against the sky had to be the broad crest of the ridge they'd been climbing for the past century. It wasn't more than a hundred yards ahead, another couple minutes of tiresome plodding.

Right and left, this treeless high country swelled into summits. Along their crags and buttresses, the early snows were already settled in for the coming winter. With this fresh coat of white, the surrounding peaks caught the promised dawn's indirect light to glow pink and orange against a colorless sky.

Old-timers called these "the Shining Mountains," and Fargo could see why. Even Sedgwick was looking up between labored footsteps. Soon they all halted, for they had gained the broad and grassy saddle. They seemed to be standing on an island that had been thrust up from a sea of swirling darkness that filled the valleys that plunged ahead and behind.

"Take a break," Fargo announced. "But don't sit down." He looked straight at Sedgwick, who responded with a vacant stare and a dopey grin. "Had enough trouble getting you up last time you sat down."

Sedgwick sighed and nodded. Polly smiled, and even managed to utter a sensible thanks after Fargo fished some jerky out of his saddlebags and passed it around.

By the time they finished chewing the jerky and draining a canteen, there was enough light for a better view ahead. The pack trail that climbed Mosquito Pass zigzagged directly under them. The pass itself, little lower than its flanking ridges, crossed to their right, perhaps a mile off. Beyond the pass, rising from the far side of the next valley, a great wall of massive gray mountains caught the morning light.

A painstaking hour of dreadful sidehilling got them to the pass, a gap in the ridge that held perhaps a foot of snow. Behind them, over toward Pikes Peak, which was quite clear even though it was a hundred miles away, the sun was starting to get serious about rising. Before them, the trail plunged into shadows, cork-screwing its way down the steep, barren slope. The placer mining camp of Oro City lay only a few miles ahead.

The going was easier now, much easier. With every step, the path improved. Sedgwick breathed more freely when he was going downhill. The sun hadn't made a formal appearance yet, but the turquoise sky gave ample light. Although they were still above timberline, prospect holes dotted the hillsides. Perhaps a mile ahead, and several hundred feet below them, the trees stood tall. It looked like a sensible place to rest for a spell.

From there on in to Oro, they could ride their mounts. And from there? Polly could doubtless practice her profession there, or just about anywhere she took a mind to. Eyeing her appreciatively, even though the long night trip had taken most of the sassiness out of her step, Fargo knew she carried all the tools of her trade.

As for Sedgwick, his ranch sat less than twenty miles from Oro City. The ragtag mining camp flanked California Gulch, a couple miles above its junction with the Arkansas River. The cowboy could follow the low river to his ranch—his for the rest of the month, anyway—and explain to his sisters-in-law why their husbands would never return.

As Fargo peeled gear off the horses and turned them loose to graze in the lush grass that lapped at the red-barked spruce, he studied on his next step. He, too, could follow the Arkansas south. In about sixty miles, where the river turned east, a well-worn trail continued south. It crossed gentle Poncha Pass and dropped into the vast and flat but mountain-rimmed San Luis Valley.

There the Rio Grande started. It flowed to Santa Fe, to El Paso and beyond, down so far south that snow was only something people read about in books. They weren't even all that familiar with frost. Savoring the thought of a winter in Texas, the Trailsman leaned back against his unrolled bedroll and drifted off to sleep.

Besides the sun, which had climbed about as high as it figured to get on a clear October day, everything looked pretty much the same. Curled up in her borrowed ankle-length wool coat, Polly must have been enjoying her dreams, because she was smiling. Stretched out like a hide being dried, Sedgwick no longer breathed hard; it was more like a gentle snore. The horses grazed placidly. Only the Ovaro bothered to perk up its ears when Fargo rose and stretched.

No matter how much he stretched, the kinks remained in his calves and the knots refused to leave his thighs. Six or eight hours of small, slow steps will do that, he figured. The only cure was a few minutes of long, fast strides.

At the edge of the grove, Fargo stepped across the tiny creek, then up a grassy hillside. A house-sized outcrop of gray-blue rock looked like as good a goal as any before he turned around and returned to his nap.

Fargo was just a few yards short of the outcrop when he heard the first shot. He was on his belly, reaching for the Colt, when the second and third sounded, then echoed on the rocks and cliffs.

The sounds were sharp, precise, which meant that the gun wasn't far away. But they came fast, too fast for a single-shot rifle. Warily, he turned his head. Puffs of gray smoke uphill drifted into the cloudless sky. Big puffs, too big for a pistol.

Must be one of those newfangled Henry repeating rifles. The idea was good, even if the weapon did jam too often to suit a man whose firearms had to be absolutely reliable. Wishing he had his trustworthy Sharps carbine in hand, Fargo crawfished, trying to get a more comfortable view of his assailant's perch. His movement attracted more shooting.

Whoever was up there wasn't much of a shot. Three rounds whizzed by harmlessly overhead. The fourth hit the ground a yard away from the Trailsman's shoulder, then ricocheted with a whine as it skipped on downhill.

But that was small comfort. The shots had come in a staccato burst. Even a blind pig finds an acorn every now and again, though. Even a piss-poor marksman might hit his target if he could throw enough lead at it. And it was plumb amazing how many rounds that fellow could lever in and trigger in just a few seconds.

If this lead-slinger couldn't hit a stationary target, though, he'd likely have more trouble with a moving one.

Fargo sprang up like a jackrabbit. Twisting to his left, he jolted four paces, then cut right, straight uphill for five. Left again for three at a slower clip. Skip right for seven. Even though bullets flew on both sides, he kept track of the count of his steps. It was the only way to remain unpredictable. Otherwise, habit would take over and establish a pattern. In these situations, the most predictable thing about predictable men was that they became dead men.

The marksman stood straight, gun to his shoulder as he levered in round after round. Not more than thirty yards distant, up above the outcrop, the smoking barrel of the Henry swung in halting arcs. If the man holding it had ever bothered to take his time, he might have drawn a decent bead on his shifting target.

Drawing his Colt as he legged closer, Fargo stopped on tiptoes and sidestepped. He didn't expect his snap shot to hit anything except the thin air, and it didn't. But it did give the jittery rifleman something new to worry about.

The next two shots from the Henry sailed high—a common problem for folks shooting downhill. Now the man was more than a silhouette against the sky. He wore baggy miner's pants, held up by rope suspenders. He had a red beard, and sported a black and battered derby hat. Husky, muscular and at least six feet tall, he had all the makings of a tough opponent in hand-to-hand combat.

But his brawny arms shook too much now to be of much help in this fight. As Fargo zigzagged closer, he levered the Henry again, and pulled the trigger. Nothing happened, except that he cussed and dropped flat behind a few low rocks.

Fargo joined in the cussing and dropping flat when the barrel of another Henry poked out and started barking.

After three harmless shots, the man finally said something.

"It'll cost you your life, asshole, if you come any closer."

"It'll cost you yours if I get any closer."

"That's as may be. But you ain't gonna take my claim whilst I'm alive to stop you."

"Damn right," Fargo shouted back. "I don't want your goddamn claim."

Silence settled over them. The rustling grass and the babble of the creek reached Fargo's ears. The sulfurous smell of powder smoke drifted off. A sharp chunk of rock chewed at the Trailsman's belly. Just inches from his face, an ant crawled up his arms, headed for the Colt he held with both hands. Fargo's second puffing effort sent the tiny critter flying back into the short grass.

"Mebbe you don't want my claim, personal. But that son of a bitch you work for sure wants to jump it."

"You got it wrong," the Trailsman shouted back. "I'm just passin' through." He sidled over a foot or two so that some new rock could poke at his flesh. Glancing toward the corners of his vision, nowhere could he see any decent cover. Just fist-sized rocks sprinkled among the short grass. He'd have to stay low until this forted-up miner ran out of lead or acquired some common sense.

"I know what you are. You're one of them gunslicks he said he'd sic on me. But I ain't givin' up without a fight."

"You know more'n I do, then. Like I said, I'm just passin' through."

"You ain't fixin' to take my mine?"

"Mister," Fargo explained, "all I want is away from here. I'd be mighty pleased if I could just mosey down to those trees, get the other folks, and ride on out of here. Far as I'm concerned, you can keep diggin' on your mine till you come out in China."

"Other folks? What other folks?"

"A friendly lady and a cowboy from hereabouts."

The stentorian voice got friendlier but retained its edge of suspicion. "Tell me who he is. If it ain't a name I know, I'll reckon you're lyin' to me some more."

"Sedgwick. Jim Sedgwick. Tall, skinny kid, gangly. Still plenty wet behind the ears, but if he lives through it, likely he'll make a pretty good man."

"That's him all right. He tell you anything about a banker named Griswold?"

"While we were in jail together in Buckskin Joe."

The Henry's barrel sagged. "Shit, why didn't you say so at first? I didn't know we was on the same side. And I surely do hate havin' to shoot at folks."

"You ain't very good at it, either." Keeping his Colt carefully pointed toward the prone rifleman, Fargo got to his feet.

So did the barrel-chested miner, who kept his empty hands and baritone voice up and friendly. "Name's George Woods." He reached to shake, and Fargo holstered his Colt.

"Fargo. Skye Fargo."

"I've heard of you."

"Don't hold any of it against me."

The fiery-haired miner laughed. "Mostly it was good. And you can't take what you hear too serious, anyhow." Suddenly his ruddy face paled, and he gulped and swallowed some. "Mister, I hope you don't take it personal that I was shootin' at you."

"Only if you'd hit me. Hope you're better at hitting pay dirt than you are at hitting targets."

They stood silently for a moment. Fargo followed the man's eyes to his mine workings, such as they were. They stood on a rolling prominence, just above timberline. On one side, the house-sized outcrop of blue-gray rock jutted out; below it sat the grove with Fargo's companions. On the other side of their hill, directly opposite the outcrop, there was a small log cabin, next to a pile of shattered waste rock. "You've got a tunnel there?" Fargo asked.

"Not much of one," Woods confessed. "Barely stand straight in it. And it likely won't belong to me much longer."

"Why's that?"

"Banker Griswold." The man sighed. "Got a jug down there. We could sit a spell while I tell you about it, if you're of a mind to listen. Couldn't blame you if you wasn't, though."

"Let's fetch the jug and go to my camp to study on it. The folks I'm with might get edgy if they wake up and I'm not around. And that Sedgwick kid does somethin' stupid every time he gets edgy. He might get proddy if he doesn't get a chance to top your sad tales about banker Griswold."

Woods laughed and said that was fine with him. They legged it down to the cabin, the miner toting his empty Henry. While he stowed it and found the jug, Fargo looked around the mine.

It wasn't much. A tunnel, needing more timbering than it had, extended back into the hillside. The hole wasn't more than a yard wide, if that, and Fargo couldn't have stood straight in it. Along its rough floor, a series of battered planks extended into the darkness. This operation wasn't even big enough to support a tramcar with rails; the rock got mucked into the rusty wheelbarrow that was propped next to the portal.

"No, the R-A-M don't look like much," Woods conceded as they hoofed it up the slope toward his good Henry.

"Three letters? Funny name for a mine."

"Horse pitched me up here and I slid a good ways on the rocks, tearin' the butt off my trousers. But the claims recorder said it wasn't proper to name it the Ragged Ass Mine, so we settled for initials."

Woods moved along at a good clip, fast enough for Fargo to feel light-headed again. "Funny you're tunneling. Isn't this placer country?"

"It was. The gravel at California Gulch is starting to run mighty thin, though. Wasn't near as many men here this summer as last. Oro City never was much of a city, an' it's gettin' to be less of a town every day."

And in a hundred years, maybe, the trees and grass would return to the once-beautiful little valley. But until every possible morsel of gold had been scooped up, the creek would run filthy, its gouged banks stripped of their cover. If possible, the adjoining settlement was even filthier than the creek and uglier than the gulch.

They paused at the crest for Woods to grab his other rifle. As they loped down, the miner continued his story.

"All them sluices down at Oro kept getting clogged up with heavy black sand. No gold in it, so nobody never paid no never mind to it. It was just a goddamn nuisance. But I got curious and melted some in a skillet one night. It's carbonate of lead, and there's whole mountains of it here."

"Thought you was usin' bullets mighty freely," Fargo replied.

"Ain't just that. Even if it was pure lead, the cost of shipping it to anywhere from here wouldn't make mining it pay. But there's considerable silver in it. So I worked my way up to this outcrop"—he waved his hand at it as they went by—"and figured my best chance of striking the vein was comin' in from the other side with a tunnel. It's lookin' good, damn good. Might have been the salvation of Oro City."

Sedgwick and Polly were on their feet, although yawning. The lanky cowboy carried an armload of branches, and Polly was still assembling kindling inside a fire ring of blackened stones. The cowboy and the miner had at least a nodding acquaintance, and Fargo completed the introductions.

By the time Woods resumed his story, they had a crackling fire. The jug was moving around, but not as fast as the smoke shifted. No matter where you sat, it would find your face and start choking your nostrils and filling your eyes with tears.

Even at that, the fire provided more cheer than Woods. He swigged at least a finger's worth of fiery corn liquor out of the unlabeled jug, and looked at Sedgwick. "Heard you had a set-to with ol' Griswold, too. Lemme tell you what happened to me."

Fargo yawned and got comfortable as the jug went to Polly, who sipped rather daintily, and then to his own hand.

"Wouldn't be so bad if I'd gone to the son of a bitch beggin' for money. But he come to me. Said he'd heard I was onto somethin', somethin' that might keep Oro City from dryin' up an' blowin' away after the placers pinch out. I said that might be the case, but we'd both end up happier if'n he'd just mind his own business."

Woods belched and wiped his hairy mouth with the sleeve of his patched and faded flannel shirt.

"So he said it could be his business, because he had substantial investments hereabouts, and he wanted the place to grow and prosper and all that. With some capital, which he could line up, we might develop my prospect into a big-time silver mine."

Fargo nodded, then prodded with, "There are limits on what a man can do with a pick, shovel, and wheelbarrow."

"Don't I know. Anyhow, he kept at me, sayin' how rich we could all get. I figured I'd just go my own poor, stupid way, though. I'd pack the best ore over the pass to Alma, an' then the wagon freighters could get it to Denver, where they can refine it decent. You wonder where all them old-time pirates went? They're wagon freighters now. But even payin' a hundred dollars a ton, all told, I was comin' along okay. An' then old Griswold foreclosed on the freight outfits."

Sedgwick nodded expectantly and muttered, "That son of a bitch."

Thus encouraged, the miner went on. "He gets a monopoly on the freighting, and then doubles my rates—nobody else's, of course. Coupla good old boys tried to start their own outfit last summer, an' they run into a suspicious-like 'accident' that killed 'em both. So old Griswold got me by the balls—'scuse me, ma'am—an' then he started twistin'."

Polly said he didn't need to watch his language on her account, and snuggled close to Fargo, boredom showing on her face. Like bartenders, whores tended to hear more hard-luck stories than anybody ought to.

" 'Course I needed credit once he started high-jackin' me on freight rates, an' of course he was willin' to give it to me. An' then when a load somehow gets lost a couple weeks ago, he says he still needs to be paid for tryin' to ship it, an' of course it didn't get to the smelter, so I ain't got no money to pay for it. So he announces he's got a lien on my property, an' he'll send some men up to take it over less'n I provide some cash. Such cash as I had went straight into some serious shootin' hardware. I ain't about to hand over somethin' I've busted my back on to some bastard that ain't never lifted nothin' heavier'n a quill pen."

"He don't lift many mortgages, that's for sure," Sedgwick interjected.

"And you started shooting at me this afternoon because you thought I was one of his boys," Fargo said.

Polly straightened and looked up at Fargo, her face ashen. "You mean there really was shooting? I thought it was part of a dream."

Woods laughed and explained, apologizing again to Fargo for the misunderstanding. Then he and Sedgwick started comparing notes on Rufus Griswold, while Polly rustled some lunch. Leaning back while the conversation droned on about other folks' difficulties with the banker, Fargo studied on the view to the west.

The Mosquito Pass road dropped down to Oro City. Although they couldn't see the settlement, it couldn't be more than four or five miles away. Across the Arkansas River, gigantic peaks loomed, climbing considerable heights above timberline. The upper parts showed a patchwork of bare pinkish-gray granite and shimmering fresh snow.

No surprises there, but there was something worrisome behind those summits. Clouds black as coal had piled up against the far side of the Sawatch Range. Although the sky was deep blue and warm overhead, that could change within minutes if that storm managed to get over the mountains.

So Fargo didn't mind a bit when Woods announced it was time to go back to mucking with occasional breaks to shoot at any of Griswold's men that might be coming. Already the shadows were getting long, and by the time they rode into Oro City, most of the afternoon had passed.

7

Oro City had slipped plenty since its glory days, which were only a year in the past. During the preceding summer, its main street had been bustling, day and night. New buildings had gone up as fast as the lumber could be sawed and delivered. Drunken men swaggered up and down the street, bragging on the wealth of their claims and showing off fair-sized nuggets they'd just fetched out of California Gulch.

After two years of such feverish activity, the gulch still held some gold. Enough to keep a few men working their sluice boxes and long toms, but all the easy stuff had been taken. Listless dogs slept in the rutted street. Half the buildings stood empty and abandoned; many had been stripped for firewood.

For a few minutes, Fargo judged the livery stable to be one of those. But some hollering finally brought the bowlegged, wizened hostler around. The elderly gent couldn't decide whether he admired Polly or the Ovaro more. Polly solved that problem for him by wandering off. Sedgwick had already decided to ride on home, figuring that if he could cross the mountains on a dark night without a trail, likely he could find a ranch in a valley when the route was familiar.

"Don't want to stable my pinto," Fargo explained. "I just want him grained, and I want to buy some oats, too. And I need to stock up my own supplies, because I figure to be somewhere else when winter arrives here."

"You seen them ugly clouds to the west, too?" The old-timer ran his finger along the ledger and silently mouthed some numbers. It was touch-and-go as to whether he'd have to take off his boots to count to twenty. Then he looked up again. "Lemme see. Ol' Hod Tabor done closed his store an' moved over to Buckskin Joe. Up an' comin' place. Ever been there?"

Taking Fargo's noncommittal stare for an answer, the codger continued. "Don't blame him a bit. Ain't much left here. But it does complexicate buyin' stuff here, without no general store. Might check at the hotel. Likely they'll sell you what you need out of their kitchen." He squeezed his eyes together, evidencing the mental work required for him to think more than five minutes ahead. "And if I ain't about when you finish them errands, just fetch your horse and head south. Wish I was goin' with you."

If any further evidence of Oro City's decline was needed, the combination hotel-saloon-restaurant provided it. The town's only two-story building was well-nigh deserted. Fargo ordered bourbon and a steak, then jawed some with the dark-bearded bartender about buying some traveling grub.

"Sounds reasonable to me. But you'll have to take that up with Cookie. He'll be free soon as he's made your dinner." The bartender's dark eyes widened and his brows lifted. "Mister, I surely do hope you're ready for what's comin' through the door. It don't look like they're friends that are about to call on you." Then he ducked and got comfortable.

Fargo had already figured as much, since a mirror hung behind the bar. There were three of them. Somebody trying to decide which one was the ugliest would have faced a difficult decision.

The middle one, a huge, lumbering man whose bald dome was fringed with greasy gray hair, sported a sneer so cold and arrogant that his crooked red nose really deserved to be busted again.

Two smaller vermin scuttled along at his flanks. Leftside was wiry, a scarred halfbreed who'd doubtless earned those prominent weals in knife fights. He moved smooth and slinky, wasting no motion. Rightside had to be the gunman of the trio, considering the low and serious way he wore a pistol on each hip.

Fargo turned slowly as they stopped in the middle of the room. "You boys the welcoming committee for

Oro City? Or do you know something that I should know about?"

The big one did the talking. "You're the one that rode in on that Ovaro, ain't you?"

"Could be," Fargo admitted. "Is there a problem?"

"Not unless you plan on riding out on that pinto."

The Trailsman smiled. "Well, that is my plan."

Big guy turned to Gunhand. "This feller's kind of dense, ain't he? Anybody with a lick of brains would know better'n to ride into our town with fine horse-flesh and fine womanflesh, if'n he wanted to keep 'em both."

"Guess I am kind of stupid," Fargo conceded. "So mayhaps one of you smart gents can answer a dumb question for me."

Big guy's sneer returned to the Trailsman. He nodded and then grunted, "Glad to, stranger. Just ask away."

Their attention was riveted on Fargo's perplexed visage, so they didn't notice the easy way his hand was moving toward his Colt. "Simple question. Which one of you wants to die first?"

Halfbreed volunteered, sliding his right hand for the throwing knife that lurked in a sleeve sheath on his wiry left arm.

He was fast. The glistening weapon was airborne and flying true when Fargo's bullet caught him between the ears. He'd been good, too. The tip of Halfreed's knife sliced into the oaken bar and plunged in, its hilt quivering where Fargo's midriff had just been.

The Trailsman crawfished from his crouch. Goliath wasn't quite as stupid as he looked, because he'd tipped over a table and scuttled behind it. Gunhand, though, didn't figure he'd need any cover.

With his first two rounds, Gunhand punctured hell out of the cloud of Fargo's gunsmoke. The first shot demolished the mirror. But the second, lower, slammed into the bar much too close for comfort. Splinters flew into Fargo's shoulder.

Fargo's shot gained some revenge, catching Gunhand's right shoulder. The man spun; his pistol thud-

83

ded to the sawdust floor. He kept his feet under him, though, and his left hand came up with the other pistol.

The place had been dim enough before the guns filled the room with thick powder smoke. In constant motion, Fargo fired on instinct at a bobbing, reeling target.

Two shots missed. The third caught Gunhand in the side of his rib cage, spraying gore as it went in and stopped. Gunhand collapsed, just in time for Fargo to worry about something new.

A chair was coming across the room. Dodging it, Fargo hopped to one side, still bent low. But the table that came along a moment later was just too damn big to evade.

Not that Fargo didn't try. But one of its spinning legs caught his ear, knocking him back. Goliath scurried for his next missile, a whiskey bottle on the floor. Fargo's quick shot put a hole in his thigh, although the man didn't notice. The hurled bottle, cast with bruising force, crashed into Fargo's ribs and left him gasping.

It rolled into the sawdust, and so did the Trailsman. Fargo fired once more at the huge man across the room. From the sound of it, he'd nailed some flesh. But there wasn't any way to tell for sure.

Fargo's Colt was empty, and his giant opponent hadn't given up. Swinging a chair like the lion tamer at a circus, the son of a bitch was coming across the smoky room.

Heaving the whiskey bottle back as he searched for cover, Fargo caught Goliath on the forehead. From the look of it, the big guy had probably been more annoyed by mosquito bites. He just kept coming, waving that chair like a four-pronged club, grunting how he was going to teach Fargo a few lessons.

Almost flat on his back, Fargo pulled his knees up to protect his torso. He wondered how much his legs would be able to take as the chair slammed into him.

Fargo's right shin withstood the first shock as the leading legs shattered against him. The remaining jagged ends continued their arc, gouging across the calf of his other leg, leaving a trail of blood and splinters.

Such a swing left Goliath open for a moment. Lashing forward, Fargo drove his boot into the man's crotch. Reflexively, the giant clutched forward, enough for Fargo to get in another vicious kick, this time to the belly.

Goliath reeled back. With his long arms, their influence extended by the stub of a chair, he still had considerable reach on Fargo's legs. He clubbed down savagely. The chair seat slammed into Fargo's flailing shins.

Spasms of pain leaped from Fargo's legs to his brain. He shook his head, trying to come up with some way to keep from getting hammered into a bloody mush. He had the throwing knife. But it was in his boot. And if he got the boot close enough to reach, he'd leave himself open for another brutal swing. One that could break a leg, or worse.

The chair seat came down again. Gritting his teeth, Fargo kept his legs out. Meanwhile Fargo's right hand found a chunk of chair leg. It wasn't much, not much longer than his hand. Hoping to buy himself some time, he got as much arm motion as he could.

Casting the piece of wood like a spear didn't mean that it would fly true. It spun end-for-end, but stayed on course, more or less. The thing was supposed to gouge out an eye. But instead, one jagged end struck where the big man's eyebrows came together.

That helped, though. The bald man roared something about how Fargo would have to pay for blinding him. His problem wasn't quite that serious, though. His eyes were just full of blood, as he'd discover as soon as he tried wiping them with his dirty sleeve.

Taking advantage of the lull, Fargo crawfished through the wood fragments and arrived at Gunhand. The fellow had bled profusely, but was still moving some. Not enough, though, to prevent Fargo from grabbing one of his revolvers.

The big son of a bitch cleared his eyes in time to see Fargo bring the gun up. He leaped, heading straight for the Trailsman. Fargo's shot was quick and accurate, right into the center of the man's bald spot.

But even dead men can have momentum. His tremendous weight slammed against the crouching Fargo and rolled him back to the floor.

When Fargo came around, he wanted to shoot again. At that worthless bartender. It was bad enough that the shithead let his local customers come in and abuse strangers. It was even worse that the gutless wonder hid behind the bar while that happened, even though he had to be handy to a greener, or a heavy bung starter, or some other way of discouraging assaults.

But the man's major crime was how he roused such victims as might be living. There just wasn't any call for emptying a pitcher of flat beer on a knocked-out man.

Spluttering and shaking as he sat up, Fargo restrained his impulse to kill, or at least seriously maim, the bartender. There were too many people standing around. One of them extended a hand to help him stand up.

On his feet and grateful, although he still felt queasy and light-headed, Fargo blinked and got used to the idea. He looked for his benefactor, and had to look down.

Quite a ways down. The crown of the man's derby barely reached Fargo's shoulders. Fargo stepped back for a better view. This fellow wore a broadcloth suit, complete with a vest. He might have come up short in the stature department, but he was built stout, with wide shoulders. The clothes fit him well, so they had to be custom-tailored to hang suitably on such an odd frame. Which meant that the thin-faced man with the waxed mustache had some money.

He and Fargo looked at each other before Fargo broke the silence. "Thanks for the hand. You're the first person around here who's tried to help me up, instead of down."

The man smiled and offered to shake. "You're welcome. And if you feel up to it, I'd like to talk to you."

Fargo felt as if there were arms, soft arms but still very powerful, reaching up from the floor, trying to grab him and pull him back down there. Just standing and focusing his eyes was getting to be a lot more work than it generally was. "Be glad to," he finally said, "if we can do it while I'm sitting down and eating the damn steak I ordered when I came in here."

The dapper man nodded, then turned to the bartender. "Get us both big steaks with all the trimmings. Put it on my account, of course." He started walking toward a corner table; the onlookers parted and Fargo followed.

They got comfortable within moments as a bottle of bourbon arrived with two shot glasses. Fargo decided that it wouldn't be so bad if his throbbing legs went ahead and fell off, if only that would make them stop hurting so bad.

"I don't know who you are," the man said after they'd both wet their whistles. "But anybody that got rid of those three worthless louts is a benefactor to this community. And any man who managed to take them all on and come out alive is a man I'd like to have on my side. Would you be looking for work?"

"That's flattersome," Fargo agreed, "but I'm just passing through, on my way to someplace warm to winter. Had a bellyful of these mountains."

Across the small table, the man poured another shot before replying. "I can understand that. Up here, we've got nine months of winter and three months of cold weather. If summer doesn't come on a Sunday, most folks miss it. But I believe I could make it worth your while to stay and work for me."

"Doubt it." The Trailsman eyed his whiskey and decided he'd had enough. There were too many other things tonight—the thin air, his loss of blood, the recent fight—that tended to blur a man's thinking. He needed to keep his wits about him. "But you're welcome to try as long as I'm sitting here drinking your whiskey and eating your food."

The man laughed. "Fair enough." Their steaks arrived before he got much further, but afterward, he started talking, with the tone of a man who didn't get interrupted much.

His problem was fairly simple. A lot of people owed him money and didn't want to pay. Or weren't able to. Which meant going after the collateral. Which was tricky in this country where folks tended to shoot quickly whenever somebody came near their property. The local law, being elected by those folks, didn't help worth mention.

"I believe I've heard of you," Fargo finally interjected. "You'd be Rufus Griswold, wouldn't you?"

Griswold nodded, his mustache bristling as his face paled. "I wasn't going to bring that up quite so soon. But I'll ask you to hear me out. Please don't prejudge me merely on the basis of what you may have heard."

Fargo found a toothpick and put it to work. "You've been civil to me. I'd feel lower'n a snake in a well if I couldn't do the same for you."

The banker took the long view of things. Placer mining chewed up valleys in a hurry as miners scrambled through the gravel. Within a year or two, the easy pickings were gone. But the flecks and nuggets of gold that landed in creeks had to wash down from somewhere upstream, where rich veins of ore came to the surface.

To extract the precious metals from the veins meant extensive shafts and tunnels, as well as grinding mills, separation tanks and chemicals, smelters, and a lot of other expensive equipment. To get gold out of a creek, a prospector could carry all the gear he needed on his burro, and the whole outfit wouldn't cost more than a hundred dollars. To get gold out of the mountain took thousands of dollars.

"You don't raise that kind of money around here," Griswold explained. "It takes investors from Boston and New York and London. But they aren't about to risk their money, no matter how much silver and gold there is around here, if they can't be sure of a few things."

"Not many certainties around here," Fargo commented dryly.

"But things could be considerably more stable," the banker continued. "You've got no law to speak of here." He pointed to the door, where the last of the three bodies was being dragged out. "Those oafs have been terrorizing strangers here for six months, and you're the first to stop them. There isn't clear title to most of the claims and land around here. People default on their mortgages all the time, and then wonder why nobody bothers to lend them more money."

Griswold looked exasperated, but before Fargo could get in a word, he just kept going.

"I believe this area could have a great future. Those mountains are rich. But it will never develop that promise without some stability. And you look like just the man to help me bring in some order. With some investment, they'll be mining here for centuries. With no investment, Oro will be a ghost town in a year. Buckskin Joe might last three or four. Breckenridge perhaps five. I've invested a lot of my life and hard work up here. So have many other people. And we're going to lose it all unless there's some order and stability in these mountain towns."

By the time the banker wound down, his after-dinner talk sounded more like a sermon. Fargo didn't take kindly to being preached to, but he didn't mention that. The Trailsman also kept in mind that the polite gent across the table was about as greedy and ambitious as men could get, but he didn't mention that, either. Best not to make more enemies hereabouts unless it was absolutely necessary.

"Mr. Griswold, I don't know enough to argue one way or the other over what you just said. But I do know that I don't much care for mining camps. Especially ones that get bitter cold and snowbound for most of the year. I was on my way to Texas, and I can't see any reason to change course."

Griswold leaned back and appeared to accept Fargo's refusal. But he had to give it one more try. He slid the chair back and jumped to his feet.

"I know you must have heard some awful things about me. How I'd foreclose on my own mother. Look at me. Do you see horns and a tail? Am I holding a pitchfork? No, I'm just a man that believes this place might have a future if people acted sensibly and politely and kept their promises. That's all. Sure you won't reconsider?"

Fargo pushed his own chair back and stood, slowly. "I'm sure. It's not my line of work, and there's a storm coming. I mean to get on my way. But I do thank you for the meal."

Griswold sighed and sat back down, propping his head in his hands. Fargo figured the easiest way to find the cook and see about some traveling grub was to go out the front door and get around to the back door.

Outside, the air felt damp, clammy. It was cool, but not the crisp chill of the preceding night. No stars twinkled in the sky; the clouds had arrived. Muttering a curse, the Trailsman started around the building.

"Hey, Fargo." It was Woods, the miner. "You workin' for him now?"

Fargo turned to the sound in the shadow. "No. I'm just looking for the cook."

"That ain't funny, Fargo," Woods hissed.

Something rustled to the rear. Fargo spun on his feet, drawing as he turned. Pinwheels and skyrockets exploded in his head, starting somewhere near his right ear.

8

No colors. No glowing red, no solemn blue, no cheerful yellow, no vibrant green. Just black and white and every possible shade of gray, as if the world had been reduced to a charcoal sketch.

Indirect hazy light entered the chamber from a typical ranch-house window—half a dozen clear whiskey bottles, their tapered tops snapped off cleanly by a woman who knew the trick with candle and string. Despite the fresh chinking around the primitive window's rough-hewn frame, bitter outside air found its way into the room.

Not that the vicious drafts entered a real room. This was a corner of a log cabin, set apart from the rest by two sheets of frayed and faded wagon canvas. Perhaps seven feet square, the cubicle was just barely big enough to encompass some gear on the floor, along with the big man's spread-out bedroll.

Skye Fargo tugged at his bedroll as he burrowed deeper inside it. Not that it mattered. A polar bear didn't have enough of a pelt to avoid these drafts. No matter how much he shifted and twisted and started to think he was comfortable, the icy knives penetrated.

At least the cold seemed real. All the rest—the two log walls joining at a rude corner, the translucent window with its indistinct gray light, the canvas curtains, the utter lack of color—had the quality of a dream. Or maybe whatever happened to folks after they died.

Fargo stuck his head out, looked up and around again, and studied on that notion. It was too damn cool, almost cold, despite the comforting weight of the blankets. There was some smoke scent, but certainly nothing acrid like brimstone. There were muffled sounds, but none resembled weeping or wailing or gnashing of teeth.

The visible world presented a cloudy, ethereal aspect. Here a man might expect to see folks sporting wings and strumming harps. But that didn't add up either. Try as he might, the Trailsman couldn't recollect any shoot-out at the Pearly Gates. And that was the only way he'd get inside.

Limbo, maybe? Whatever that was. A priest down by Santa Fe had once mentioned somesuch. But they'd downed considerable wine by the time the conversation got to such matters, and their drunken talk really hadn't been worth remembering, even if the Trailsman could recall it.

Fargo shook his head. It still seemed to be there. But his brain wasn't working worth mention. He couldn't get his thoughts in order. Drowsy and groggy, he inhaled deeply and sat up. Just about then, the cabin rattled with a gust and a river of frosty air cascaded through the makeshift window and attacked his bare shoulders.

The Trailsman spied his wool shirt in the clutter next to his bedroll. It just made sense to put some clothes on before finding out what might be going on over on the other side of the canvas curtains. He already had a fair idea what was happening on the other side of the logs. A roaring early blizzard, which would complicate hell out of getting to Texas in time to miss the rest of what promised to be an especially vicious Rocky Mountain winter.

As Fargo pulled the shirt over his shoulder, grimacing at the way the rough, cold cloth scraped at his scars, the curtains parted.

The barefoot woman wasn't much bigger than a minute. She'd have to stand twice to cast a shadow. Even so, she had a considerable shape. She wasn't wearing much of anything beneath her ankle-length flannel nightshirt, and it bulged in all the right places— more than stood to reason, up near the top, unless she was nursing a little one.

Ash-blond hair came down to her shoulders and just

kept falling. The pale face looked tired and weathered. Her thin lips were clenched with the same energy that she also applied to her two-handed grip on a two-foot-long stove poker.

"You're awake," she muttered. "And I'm ready for you."

Fargo rubbed his sore temple while various other aches and pains announced their presence. "I can't say I'm ready for that." He gestured toward the poker and continued wrestling with the shirt. "I hurt all over already, and I've been out cold for a spell. If it's all the same to you, I'd just as soon not try that again."

The woman let the poker's bent end land on the splintery plank floor, then released it so it leaned against the canvas wall before she bent and grabbed the hem of her nightgown. Straightening, she gathered the garment and heaved it over her shoulders. In two quick steps, she was standing on the bedroll.

"Like what you see, Mr. Fargo?"

The woman was so short that Fargo could reach her shoulders with his hands, even though he was still sitting on the floor. A tiny woman with huge breasts and dark nipples, her plump belly contrasted with her thin shoulders and sharp collar bone. He pulled her down onto his lap and held her there for a moment. She felt real enough. She looked real enough.

Feeling oddly winded, the Trailsman avoided the impulse to gasp. He breathed slowly and deeply while the woman's pale blue eyes moved from his head to his toes, and back again. Maybe he was in heaven after all. Or it was some nasty trick of the devil's. Fargo waited tensely.

"Mr. Fargo, you took away my man," she said.

And suddenly Fargo had a solid idea of where he was and who she was. Anna Sedgwick, he realized, remembering Jim's stories in prison. She was the widow of one of the bank robbers he had shot. But if she held that against him, she certainly had a peculiar way of showing it.

"You owe me," Anna murmured softly. "You've got to take his place."

"If I'm up to it," Fargo hazarded, still not entirely sure what she had in mind.

"You already are," Anna announced flatly, rubbing her derriere against Fargo's swollen organ.

There was no point in arguing with the truth. Anna's cold feet left an icy trail down the Trailsman's thighs and calves as she snuggled and pushed him backward. Then she started undoing those buttons that had been so difficult for Fargo to fasten just a few minutes earlier.

As she took off his shirt, Fargo shivered. The cold draft from behind him matched anything Canada might have to offer. Quickly, he slid under the covers with Anna. Fargo's hands moved around to massage her writhing back, drawing her heated body closer.

"Oh, Jesus," she muttered. "You can't know what it was like, just seeing you here, and me feeling so empty and not able to do anything about it."

Men spent considerable time yearning and dreaming; he knew what it was like. He just wished he could be sure he wasn't merely dreaming then and there. Anna pressed her taut, swollen breasts against him. Now that they were both ready, she wasn't going to waste any time.

Tiny as she was, the widow Sedgwick no doubt would have felt uncomfortable smothered under a man as big as Fargo. So she just wiggled down, slipping her hips back and forth, spreading her warm thighs along the way, until her unfilled moistness snagged the tip of Fargo's erect shaft.

Whether she was an angel or a dream, everything from her cold feet to her heated center kindled a response. And Anna obviously figured on getting the most from him, too, for when Fargo surged upward, so did she, continuing to gyrate as she rose with him. She rotated smoothly, massaging her cleft with his organ and moaning all the while.

Fargo sank back, then prodded deeper, sliding into place.

"Oh yes," she groaned, "don't waste any of it. Slow, slow, slow."

"At your service, ma'am," Fargo replied, moving

94

one hand to cup a breast, the erect nipple pushing through between his fingers. A man had to study on something to slow things down. If his thoughts moved any farther down her flushed body, he'd start getting in too much of a hurry to pleasure her in the leisurely way she wanted to be pleasured.

Fargo raised his hips, his energy focusing on penetrating deeper, but she slid upward, maintaining the general distance. Without breaking their up-and-down rhythm, though, she allowed Fargo farther in. But it was at her unhurried pace that he moved deeper and deeper.

That went on for far longer than seemed reasonable, but Fargo wasn't complaining.

Especially not when she bent low and pressed her torso against his, her bottom still twitching and writhing. "Oh, Mr. Fargo, I've got all of you in me now," she gushed. "Just keep it there, keep me full."

Fargo pushed higher. She panted feverishly before gasping. "You mean there's more?"

The Trailsman's actions spoke more directly than any words could have.

As if some spring had been released inside her, she bolted upright. She hadn't known the half of Fargo until gravity took over and pulled her the rest of the way down his shaft.

"It ain't right," she hollered. "I thought you was a regular man, not a two-legged stud horse. There ain't room," she moaned as Fargo surged upward. "But I want more," she breathed, pushing herself down on his lap, her muscles drawing tight around his shaft. "Harder," she commanded. "Push harder."

His hands now slid slowly from her bobbing breasts to her heaving shoulders. Firmly and deliberately, Fargo pushed her down against his groin. It was like trying to put a cork back into a bubbling champagne bottle, the way they were both fixing to explode, but he maintained the pressure, intensifying the force from above as he increased the pressure from below.

"Oh God, now, now, now!" Anna shouted, rearing up over him, oblivious to the rush of cold air that poured from the drafty window frame. She'd been the one who wanted to take things slow and easy, though, so Fargo rocked for a minute or two enjoying the view.

Silken thighs spread toward him, merging in a glistening thatch that swayed atop his jingling balls. The swell of her hips that engorged him, tapering to a high waist, her navel almost motionless as though it were the center that the rest of her revolved around. The outlines of her heaving ribs just barely apparent, but who'd stop to notice, what with those luscious trembling breasts to savor. And a curl-framed face that finally had some color. Lots of color, as her cheeks seemed to glow and those thin lips grew redder by the moment.

Fargo could wait no longer. He arched upward, pumping himself into her as his hands slid down to her hips and pushed her downward. They both hit bottom at the same time as she started waving and flailing.

Nestled against him after she came to her senses and realized a gal could get mighty cold, sitting exposed like that, she wrapped her small but muscular arms around his torso. "Oh, Mr. Fargo, what have I done?"

He knew she knew damn well what she'd done. "The same as anybody else does. What you felt you had to do."

"Then you'll not think less of me? I just don't know what possessed me to do what I just did—I feel so sluttish, so wanton, so . . ."

"You feel just fine," he consoled.

"But I wouldn't want you to think that I . . . that I'm one of those women. I was a proper and faithful wife. A good woman."

Anna Sedgwick squinched her face up, threatening to cry, while Fargo wondered what in hell she had been faithful to. It probably hadn't been her husband. But he didn't mind letting her play this game if she wanted to. It wasn't his place to point out that he didn't like proper women much, anyway.

"You're a good woman all right," Fargo cajoled. "Real good."

It was still damn hard for him to think straight, no doubt on account of the thin air, the way he'd lost blood lately, and the bumps on his head. But he sure didn't want to say anything foolish here. "You're smart enough to see what you want and enjoy it when you've got a chance."

"But I can't just do this," she protested, leaping up from the bedroll and standing over him as naked as a jaybird. "You took my man away from me, Skye Fargo. You killed my Sam." Before Fargo realized what was happening, Anna swooped up the discarded poker and pointed it at his belly.

"There's folks over in Buckskin that might argue that," Fargo replied cautiously, hoping this was just part of her game to reestablish herself as a good and proper woman. "I wasn't the only one shooting during that bank robbery."

"I know better. Jim told me what happened. Those men in Buckskin couldn't hit a barn door from ten paces. You know your business, Mr. Fargo." Anna stabbed the poker forward a tad. "It's just a pity that your business happens to be making happy wives into wretched widows."

"Wretched?" Fargo blurted. "You didn't seem all that wretched ten minutes ago."

"But I've been wretched for days," she argued. "And it was your work that made it so."

Anna wavered for several minutes and Fargo held his breath, although the lack of air set up a fierce pounding in his head. He could tackle her, but probably not without hurting her, and that didn't seem right after what had gone before. Finally, Anna let the sharp point of the poker drop down toward the floor.

"You seemed mad enough to kill me," Fargo commented. "Why didn't you?"

She blinked away some tears. Although Fargo still didn't believe much of her claim to being proper and respectable, the tears seemed genuine.

"There's been enough bloodshed and murder. I don't plan to use this"—she shook the poker—"unless you get out of line."

"Just what would that mean?"

Her words came deliberately as she eased her grasp on the rod of iron in her tiny hands. "You don't do anything to help Mr. Griswold. That miner, Woods, brought you down here dropped over the top of that big pinto of yours. He said you and he had disagreed some about whether you should go to work for that monster, Banker Griswold. We don't need that. We've got troubles enough as it is without you on his side. You don't cause us any more trouble. When you're able to, you move on."

"We're agreed on that, ma'am."

Anna paused. Her face looked pallid, transparent. "You'll not be heading south today. The snow's belly-deep to a big horse, and getting deeper by the minute. Jim-boy and Prudence are out there right now, trying to save such stock as we have." She looked out the window, then back at Fargo.

From behind the canvas curtain a baby cried.

The noise stopped for a moment, raising hopes that the sleeping child had merely awakened momentarily. But apparently, he was just storing up breath for an extended hungry wail.

His mother smiled at Fargo. "Little Nate. He's like every other man. When he's hungry, he hollers. And he doesn't stop hollering till he's fed. You'll excuse me?" She rose, looking embarrassed until she got inside the flannel nightshirt.

"I might start hollering myself if I don't eat soon," Fargo replied, looking for his shirt now that the more pleasant scenery was covered up. "You tend to what you've got to tend to, and I'll be out shortly."

By the time Fargo got to the cabin's main room, there was stew warming on its cast-iron stove. A few steps away, the widow Sedgwick sat on a squeaky rocking chair, cooing while she nursed the baby, with a blanket modestly draped over her shoulder. She lifted her eyes to Fargo and displayed a placid, serene look.

The headquarters of the C Bar S Ranch—that had to be its name, judging by the brand that was burned into the log walls in a couple spots—were more substantial than Fargo would have anticipated.

His makeshift chamber occupied one corner of the main room. It spread along the width of the cabin, probably thirty feet, and it was about fifteen feet deep.

Three doors, each one leading to a bedroom, opened at equal intervals along the back wall. The corners fit well and the logs had been chinked, but even so, vagrant cold drafts flitted through the room. Fargo edged over to the stove.

While enjoying the radiating heat, he tried to discern something besides whiteness as he stared through the cabin's front window, another row of bottles.

It was a wasted effort. He had to take a leak, and his Ovaro had to be out there somewhere, so he nodded at the widow and headed for the door. There was nothing else to do.

9

A palpable blast of vicious wind full of eye-stinging particles almost pushed him back. It whipped the door from his hand and slammed it around. Like a night-hawk raiding crew, the brutal winter just stomped in uninvited.

Fargo fought back. Regaining his composure, he grabbed the plank door from the cabin wall. The door swung easily until it was halfway around, perpendicular to the wall. Then the wind started catching it.

The Trailsman got on the front side of the door and swung around, wishing he'd grabbed his coat. With his back to the wind, he managed to tug the door shut behind him before he took another look at the outdoors.

Truth be told, there was precious little to see. Just white, shimmering white. Momentary lulls in the wind displayed drifts that approached the cabin roof from this side. Ahead of him, the snow was at least waist deep as gusts swirled its surface. Fargo had seen all he needed to see.

He quickly relieved his bladder into a drift. It might have been more polite to get farther from the house, but today a man couldn't see much farther than he could reach. Getting lost and frozen to death wouldn't be difficult at all.

For an agonizing moment, Fargo feared that Anna Sedgwick had experienced a change of heart and had barred the door against his return. But he'd just pulled it so tight behind him on his way out that he had to shoulder some and argue with it to get back in.

Stomping the snow off his boots and shaking himself after another fight with the wind about whether the door could be closed, Fargo caught himself just staring at Anna Sedgwick. She looked so damn content there by the hot stove, baby at her breast while she slowly rocked. "Is it still terrible out there?" she finally asked.

"About as bad as it gets," he answered hoarsely. "Where'd you say Jim and Prudence were?"

"Tending the stock."

Fargo's eyebrows rose and she caught his astonished look. "We sold almost all our cattle, trying to pay off Banker Griswold. When this started up, Jim got most of what was left into the corral. And we have a barn next to it. It's not that big, but it'll hold the horses. That's where your pinto is. Or where I hope it is."

"So they're out in the barn?"

"Yes," she said firmly, as if saying so would make it so. "They must be. Though they've been out for several hours." Her expression fell. "Oh no. You mean that while we were in here, uh, well, while we were in here together, they could have gotten lost out there?" Anna choked back sobs. "Jim's just a boy. And Prudence, she's expecting. "Pretty far along, too." Her head dropped as she shuddered. "Oh no. How could I have just stayed in here, all warm and cozy? While they went out in that, that . . ." Her thin voice cracked and gave up on her.

"Because you were tending to that young one," Fargo told her sharply. "You were minding what you're supposed to mind. A human baby's a damn sight more important than cows and horses. They did what they thought needed to be done, and you've done what you needed to do. You've nothing to apologize for."

"I'd feel better if I could believe that."

"Then believe it."

Anna gazed at Fargo's impassive face, and her jaw quivered. "All right," she confessed. "I ain't so all-fired good. But I care about Jim and Prudence. Cared about Sam, too. I didn't want to have him die."

"I believe you," Fargo offered.

But Anna was too worked up to stop. "I guess I wasn't even real faithful," she whimpered. "But then Sam wasn't no two-legged stud horse, like you. I feel so damn guilty," she cried. "And now look what I've done. Now it's Jim and Prudence."

"Anna, your husband was trying to rob a bank. And Jim and Prudence went out there on their own. If you were the best woman in the world, you still wouldn't have a say over what other folks decide on. Don't take credit where it isn't due."

He looked around the cluttered main room. His own gear had to be stored in the barn, wherever that was. "Did they wear every stitch of winter gear when they went out?"

Instantly, he regretted asking the question, although there really hadn't been any other way to phrase it. She started sobbing, the words creeping out between whimpers. "There's Sam's stuff, back in our room."

He followed her eyes to the middle door and strode that way. There wasn't any reason to try being delicate about borrowing a coat and gloves and anything else he could find from some clothes from a man he'd killed, especially since Sam's widow wasn't exactly the delicate type. Besides, he'd already borrowed Sam's home and Sam's woman.

Sam had married. Sam had taken credit for fathering a son, although Fargo wouldn't have bet more than a quarter on the proposition. Sam had tried to build some kind of future for that boy in this high mountain valley.

Sam just might have been a decent man, a man who shouldn't have died over just one foolish notion, a quick-money scheme that was supposed to get the banker off his back so he and his kin could keep a ranch. And now Sam occupied a cold grave on the other side of the Mosquito Range, and the little boy would never know him.

As Fargo found a buffalo robe and some elk-hide gloves, he tried to tell himself what he'd just told Anna. People do what they have to do, and things often don't work the way you think they will. Worrying about it later just made it all hurt worse. No matter how much he told himself that, though, he still didn't feel much better when he got outside after another fight with the wind and the door.

Sam's coat fit tight across the shoulders, and its bottom hem no doubt rode lower when he'd been wearing it. With the hair side in, though, it was warm, and that was what mattered most.

Fargo's fingers moved stiffly, inside the tight gloves, as he adjusted his headgear—a red silk bandanna across the bottom half of his face, and a wool baby blanket wrapped around his head, tied beneath his chin. He felt himself chuckling at how he must look, but there was precious little chance of being seen.

From only a couple steps back, until the towering drifts stopped his course, the cabin was just an outline. The snow was swirling so hard that it obscured the details of the logs, and Fargo could damn near reach out and touch the wood.

Right next to the cabin, the snow was only a foot or so deep. Fargo stayed in that track, making his way around. Every time the savage wind quit howling, he turned and looked out into the milky void, hoping he'd spot the barn before the gusts started up again to block his vision.

Even if he could spot the barn, though, his troubles would just be starting. The sensible way would be to tie a long rope to the house and loop the other end around his waist. That way a man could always pull himself back home no matter how lost he got in this white wilderness.

But there hadn't been a rope inside the house. And if he was in the barn, where they kept such gear, then he'd be past needing the rope.

The Trailsman felt himself grow trembly and steadied himself with a hand on the cabin wall. He took several more steps, then waited for a lull. No barn. No nothing out there. A few more steps, and the need for patience even as the wind tried to rip the breath out of his lungs.

This was starting to look tedious, and even worse, fruitless. Maybe the barn and corral sat on the other side of a rise, where they couldn't be seen even on a clear day, let alone during this storm. Hell, this blizzard could have given lessons to any other that Fargo'd ever ventured out in, and he hadn't ever stepped more than three yards away from the cabin.

The Trailsman's probing hand, almost numb with

cold that ignored the glove, found it first. Right on the corner, where the ends of the logs stuck out, somebody had tied a lariat. Fargo tugged on it. Satisfied that the knot was secure, he stuck his right arm into one of the robe's deep pockets, looping the arm over the rope.

He followed the same process with his left arm, and told his hands that if they dared to come out of the pockets, then the rope would be dropped, and they'd all be lost and would likely freeze to death. Since they'd already been cold enough today, perhaps they'd listen.

Even cold sober, maintaining balance was tricky without any help from outstretched arms. Fargo pushed through the shoulder-high drifts next to the cabin, and felt relieved once he reached the usual stuff. It was only a hip-deep sea that swallowed every step. His tracks looked like postholes during the moments they remained visible before the wind obliterated them.

Quickening his pace, Fargo finally arrived at the end of the rope, marked by bulging knots. Good thing, or the rope might have slipped right through. And if he passed the end of this rope, he could well be at the end of his own rope. Struggling with fingers that wouldn't obey worth mention, Fargo made a loop and got the rope around his waist.

It stood to reason that the barn, or at least the privy, was within a rope's length of the house. Just which way remained a mystery—he couldn't even see the cabin—but if he kept the rope tight and went in a circle, he couldn't help but snag something.

What he'd most likely catch would be frostbite, Fargo decided after the better part of an hour, working to his right. Or he hoped he'd kept moving that way. Stumble in these drifts and get turned around, and no telling whether he was following his plans or not. Reading trail was worse than impossible when everything looked the same.

The barn almost hit him in the face. The wind had been coming so hard that he had to keep his eyes shut. And then his lashes froze together, requiring a painful effort every time he dared look around to see nothing.

Pawing at them was stupid because it could mean dropping the rope, the lifeline that he must hold.

The Trailsman's nose cleared enough to discern warm barn smells. Horse shit and rank hay smelled better than steak or even a woman's perfume as he tumbled down the front of the drift. The whipsawed plank wall in front of him was almost as blank as the field he'd just crossed. No doors, no windows, just a row of wood.

Fargo eased along the wall and turned a corner. There, a window. It was shuttered, sure enough, but he found the dexterity to open the chest-high portal and push himself inside.

Much to his surprise and pleasure, he landed in fresh hay. Moments later, Jim Sedgwick was standing over him, pulling the shutters tight. "Good to see you, Fargo," he finally said. "Better to see the rope, though."

The Trailsman sat up in the hay and collected his breath. Now he could feel icicles on his beard, tinkling against each other as he shook his head and wished that the dizzy sensation would go away. "The woman, is she all right?" he eventually asked.

Sedgwick helped get the rope off and snubbed around a stall post before answering. "She's okay." He pointed over to a head sticking out of the hay, only a couple yards away. "Warm and sleeping easy, as a matter of fact."

Fargo got a good look at Sedgwick before asking any more questions. The young cowboy was decked out pretty much like himself in a long buffalo robe, although he'd somehow managed to keep his hat on. "Glad you folks were in the barn," Fargo finally said before sagging wearily into the hay.

"Wasn't blowin' much at all when we come out this morning," Sedgwick explained. "I got the stock in whilst Pru forked hay. Thought we had it all figgered out, and then the wind come up. Damn, I wish we'd strung the snow rope when we left the house. But we didn't. And given the choice atween stayin' half warm in here, and wanderin' out there and gettin' lost in that blizzard, I didn't have to do much thinkin'."

"You did right," Fargo said. "Had us worried some,

though. Surprising you have a snow rope. That's a plains trick. Most mountain ranches don't bother."

"We come from Kansas, remember?"

Fargo nodded, then rose and found his Ovaro. The barn only seemed warm in comparison to the outdoors, the way that the pinto's breath came out in big clouds. Fargo found the bundle with his own gear and told Sedgwick it was time to get to the house.

"But the stock needs waterin'," he protested.

"The cows outside can eat snow," Fargo replied. "And the horses can manage for a day or two, till this blows over and you can let 'em out. I don't like it either, but you'd better study on somethin', kid."

Sedgwick glared and swallowed. "There a problem?"

"Like it or not, you're the man of this outfit now. You're not just a cowhand any more. You've got more on your plate now, not just the welfare of some critters, but two women, one nursin' a baby and the other carrying one. They've got to come first."

The cowboy stood straight-faced and digested the notion. "Reckon you're right, Fargo. But the usual ways of thinkin' 'bout things don't go away easy."

Sedgwick insisted on breaking trail when they followed the rope back to the house. Fargo had it relatively easy, following Prudence, but he didn't dare let the stumbling woman bring up the rear. She had to be pushed and prodded all the way.

The wind was something of a blessing because it carried off her complaints as fast as she uttered them.

Prudence Cockburn, widow of the late Red, had been sleeping warm and comfortable, and then some big rough man had roused her and pulled her to her feet and pushed her, a woman expecting a child in three or four months, head first out a window, right into a snowdrift. Then the same ogre had forced her to feel her way along a rope through the worst snowstorm that anyone had ever seen. And that worthless cousin-in-law of hers just stood there and let this all happen.

Red must have been a mighty patient man, or else he'd been deaf. There wasn't any other way to explain how he'd managed to stay around Prudence. Too tired to argue with her, Fargo just ate his stew while she railed and ranted about the unfairness of life in general, and hers in particular.

She'd been hornswoggled into marrying a no-account, who'd hauled her away from a good farm in Kansas to this godforsaken howling wilderness. Her husband was just the kind of inept lout who would manage to get himself killed robbing a bank, since he'd never done a cussed thing right. Fargo's opinion of Anna rose a few notches. She'd actually shown concern over this harpy, when the sensible thing would have been to hope the bitch froze to death.

Everyone sat around the table sheepishly hemming and hawing throughout her tirade, which continued even after the plates had been picked up. She told Anna and Jim that they were "complete and total idiots for giving shelter, and not just shelter, but board, too, to this wretched gunslinger that tried to kill off all our family. You might be fools enough to countenance this. Might, indeed. You are fools. But I, for one, see no reason to tolerate him in my sight."

Before Fargo could suggest that she shut her eyes and, more important, her mouth, Prudence stomped off to her room, shaking her close-cropped black hair with every step.

By that time, nobody else had anything to say. Fargo had trouble remembering the last time he'd felt as tired and drained as he felt now. So he wasted no time in getting to his bedroll after muttering just enough to be polite.

Perhaps it was the sudden lack of sound that brought the Trailsman to his senses while darkness still reigned outside. The wind had finally given up on hauling the mountains away and the calmness could be sensed indoors.

He sat up in his bedroll, fingers on his icy Colt as the hairs rose on the back of his neck. For what seemed an eternity, he held the position.

Then he heard shuffling noises. Silently, Fargo stood, then padded like a big cat to get as close to a canvas curtain as he could without disturbing it.

He felt the curtain flutter against his back as a shape

107

entered his chamber. There was precious little light, just enough to see a shadow. Shoulder-high and on the plump side, it held a butcher knife.

In an instant, he was behind Prudence and had her soft arms pinned to her bulging sides. Much as he cautioned himself, though, he couldn't help enjoying the way her rump rubbed against him as she wiggled in silence, trying to break his grip. But all that happened was that he tightened his hold on her right arm, increasing the pressure until the knife fell to the bedroll.

"Don't you dare try to have your way with me," she hissed.

"Not my style," Fargo whispered back. "But I'm not about to let you pick up that knife."

She stiffened. "What knife?"

Fargo pulled her against him and bent down to her ear. "You want to play games, honey, I know quite a few. But this one was old and tiresome the first time I played it. Smart as you say you are, couldn't you come up with anything better?"

She wiggled some and Fargo told his loins to ignore the sensation. "You bastard," she mumbled. "What are you planning to do?"

"Tell me your plans first, honey. It'll be the first time that I won't mind listening to you."

She tried to use her ass as a weapon, banging it against Fargo's crotch. But her rear end was just too round and soft to do any damage. "We've got to come up with money fast to save the ranch. I figured on taking yours."

Fargo made sure she could hear his chuckle. "Next thing you'll be telling me you're the good fairy. You could have taken any money I've got during the time I was planked out down there, not knowing or caring what was going on around me." He pulled her tighter against him. "Try again."

Only her heavy, labored breathing broke the silence.

"We could have some fun," Fargo told her. "Just let me drop my pants and you lift up that gown, and we're ready to go."

"In my condition?" she gasped, apparently not caring that she might wake up the rest of the house.

"We'd both enjoy it," Fargo replied. "But I suspect it'd be better if you just told me what's on your mind." He pressed forward. "You can tell what's on mine."

"You brute," she snarled. "Have you no morals?"

"Just how moral is it to go after a sleeping man with a butcher knife?"

"The man that killed my husband."

"He was robbing a bank at the time. That's not exactly something he might have learned in Sunday school."

"Let me go and I'll explain everything."

"Let you go, and if you don't grab the knife and come at me, then you'll run off screaming that I tried to rape you. Tell me why you tried to sneak up on me with that knife, honey."

Prudence tensed and tightened some more before sighing and allowing herself to relax. "I wanted to talk you into helping us. And I thought you might listen if I held a knife to your throat while I talked."

"The way you screech and ramble on about how rotten the world is, that might be the only way I'd have listened," Fargo said. "But what the hell. Try me now."

"It's hard to talk when you're holding me like this. And I feel kind of funny inside, like, well, you know. Not like talking."

"I reckon we could sit down, backs against that cold, rough wall."

Fargo kept his arm over her shoulders while she explained.

"That miner, Woods, he hates Banker Griswold just as much as we do."

"Keep going," Fargo urged. "I know that much."

"Well, just before this storm struck, he hit onto something good. Not that silver ore that he usually boasts about, but something pretty. Wire gold, I think they call it. Anyway, it's a shiny thing worth a considerable sum. He's willing to help us out of our predicament if we can help him out of his."

"Fair enough," Fargo agreed. "But it doesn't sound like he has a predicament now. Can't he just sell his gold in Oro City and go in and pay off Griswold?"

"Not exactly," Prudence explained. "Not the way he put it, anyway. There's nobody in Oro City with cash enough to pay what that's worth. Except for Griswold, of course, and you know he wouldn't pay a fair price. So Mr. Woods has to get his chunk of gold over the mountains to Denver and sell it there."

It was starting to become clear. "And Woods will come up with the rest of the cash you need to clear your title, if you can figure out a way to get his gold to Denver."

"That's it," she nodded. "Jim thinks he might be able to do it, even with all this snow." She started to shudder, now. "But Mr. Fargo, he may not be much, but he's all we have left."

"So you reckon I might be able to carry that gold across two mountain ranges and a hundred miles of snow ass-deep to a tall Indian. When I still get woozy every time I stand up, and any time I get a bump on my head, I go down and stay down for days at a stretch." Fargo sighed. "I can see now why you thought you might need that knife to persuade me."

"There was more," she added.

"More?"

"Yes. Jim says you have a reputation to maintain, so you wouldn't run off with the gold. But you're mighty fond of that horse of yours, aren't you?"

"You could say that."

"Well, I figure the horse wouldn't do you any good in all that snow, anyway. And if we keep him here, that should insure your honesty, since you'll want to come back for him."

Fargo knew that when he wanted the Ovaro, he'd come and get his horse. But it would be comforting to know that the big pinto would receive good care if he took the job.

Did he have much choice? He tried to sort out what he might or might not owe these people. It got perplexing as hell. True, they'd tended him while he'd been sick. But it was their friend Woods who'd cold-cocked him to keep him from taking a job from Griswold, which he hadn't been planning to do, anyway. These folks were just so damned suspicious, which made them act meaner than they really were. And dumber, too, dumb enough to take up bank robbery. Which got three men killed, and Fargo had fired those shots.

Damn. There wasn't any simple way to decide what to do here. No. There was. A certainty struck Fargo. Come what may, he knew that deep inside, he'd feel right if he could find a way to get the gold to Denver. He'd also feel right miserable out there in all that snow. But now he knew the answer.

"Okay. I'm not up to full speed. But I'll do it."

She started to rise, and Fargo allowed her to, bringing himself up as he did. She turned and whispered.

"Mr. Fargo, the way we were standing before?"

"What of it?"

"Could we, uh, well, damn it, could we?"

It was the first time since he'd met her that Fargo didn't feel like arguing.

10

Just getting to Oro City to find Woods and his precious cargo took the better part of two exhausting days. If the early storm had not been accompanied by wind, it would have left about four feet of snow on the level.

As it was, huge drifts rose next to cabins, fences, trees, boulders—anywhere something stuck out of the valley floor. But the winds had also scoured some areas so cleanly that clumps of brown grass showed, forming trails between great dunes of snow.

Sticking to those routes as much as he could, the Trailsman proceeded deliberately. Being in a hurry was generally a foolish notion, and never more so than now. Still weak from the lost blood, he had to husband his strength for the greater challenge that loomed to the east: the shimmering lofty wall of the Mosquito Range. Now that the sun was out, providing light but little warmth, the mountains could be blinding.

Fargo had taken precautions, fabricating some eye protection out of willow bark. His rough spectacles had no lenses, just narrow slits to allow vision while blocking most of the glare. Their refusal to sit comfortably on his nose was the biggest annoyance during the twenty miles. So he didn't see much cause to complain late in the afternoon when he reached California Gulch and trudged up the wagon road, already packed down and slick.

If Oro City had looked sickly before, the place looked dead now that it had been blanketed in deep snow. Smoke issued from perhaps a dozen chimneys of the forty or fifty structures, among them the hotel.

"You sure picked a piss-poor time to come back

from Texas," the bartender announced as he fetched some bourbon. "Must have been a fast trip, too. You were just through here right before the storm hit."

Resisting the temptation to ask "What storm?" Fargo enjoyed the whiskey's warmth on his tongue and relished the way the liquor soothed his throat on the way down. Feeling better, he finally spoke. "Short trip. Didn't even get as far south as Texas Creek, let alone the real Texas."

The edgy bartender did his best to laugh, even though it was obvious that he'd heard funnier statements. But bartenders do try to get along with any gent that walks in, kills the three town bullies, and then sits down and eats dinner while the bodies are being carted away.

"You know Woods, the miner?" Fargo asked abruptly.

"One that keeps bragging that all the black sand in the sluice boxes is really silver ore, and he's got himself a whole mountain of the worthless rock?"

"That'd be the one."

The bartender put down the glass he was washing and scratched his head. "Not seen much of him lately. Course, haven't seen much of anybody lately. Not many folks comin' through, since every damn road into or out of here is shut off."

"Even from the south?"

"Every which way. Or so I've been told. You can get around here tolerable, but there's no way into or out of this valley right now. Some men tried going north over Fremont Pass yesterday, and they came back complaining about a big snowslide blocking the canyon. To the south, Weston's worthless when there's any snow. You might get over Trout Creek Pass if you had to, I suppose, but where would you go?"

"Yeah, I've been across South Park in the winter."

"And you lived to talk about it, which is better than most do. I don't care what they say. I figure South Park doesn't really get more than a foot of snow every year, but it stays moving all the time. Those ground blizzards can be pure hell."

"It does snow sideways a lot there." Fargo poured himself another drink. "Now, how about Woods?"

"Sorry. If he's not up at his Ragged Ass Mine,

waving one of his new repeating rifles at anybody that rides by, he's likely holed up at Mrs. Jenkins's boardinghouse. It's just up the street. You can't miss it."

"One more question."

"Sure."

"Anybody around here make or sell webs?"

"Webs?"

"Snowshoes."

"Only snowshoes I ever saw anybody use weren't webbed. Norwegian snowshoes, they called 'em. They were boards that you strapped to your feet."

"New one on me." Hating the thought of leaving the whiskey and the hot stove, Fargo stepped back from the bar.

"Why for you want snowshoes, anyway?"

"Going over Mosquito Pass tomorrow."

The bartender's face went pale. "Jesus, mister. You're a dead man. Mosquito Pass kills folks by the score in the summer, what with lightning and rockslides and them godawful drops. And in the winter, it's got about a dozen other ways to kill you. Why don't you just take the bottle and go drink yourself to death? Same result, and you'll be warm and happy during your last moments."

"I'll take my chances." Fargo made his way to the door.

"You don't have any chances." The bartender might have said more, but it was lost in the rush of bone-chilling air that assaulted Fargo's ears.

Mrs. Jenkins, who couldn't have been a day over seventy, speculated that "Mr. Woods might be at the hotel, since he's enslaved by the Demon Rum, and I allow no tippling in my house. Why, I wouldn't even allow drinkers to board here, but the way things are going downhill around here, it's almost impossible to find any tenants, let alone men who don't degrade themselves. Why can't they learn to be temperate and industrious? I'm absolutely certain that their inability to find more gold is a direct result of the way they befuddle themselves. And what is that vile aroma that I smell on your breath, sir?"

"Sarsaparilla," Fargo told her. Wondering just why

a teetotaler would even consider living in a mining camp—every dismal one of them seemed perfectly designed to drive a man to drink and worse—he went back outdoors. Spotting a low-roofed shack with a trampled path to the door, he followed the path.

He might have knocked on the door, but it would have annoyed hell out of the busy folks inside. Even from the stoop, he could hear panting and giggling, along with the squeaks of active bedsprings. Easing his way in, Fargo padded through the front room, which somebody was trying to make look like a real parlor, and past the kitchen.

The bedroom door was ajar, and enough light came through the window to confirm Fargo's guess. Polly Warner was on bottom, putting on a convincing demonstration of her affection for the gent atop her. Fargo hadn't quite seen this side of her customer before, but he knew that the bobbing ass belonged to George Woods.

Facing his way, she caught the motion when the door opened more. Her eyes grew wide and her rocking slowed considerable. Fargo lifted his index finger to his pursed lips, then made thrusting and rolling motions. She got the idea and went back to work as if nothing had happened.

Too busy to notice the momentary lull, Woods was still pumping away when Fargo's hand tapped his shoulder.

The redheaded miner froze in place, then looked up haltingly. He saw the butt of Fargo's pistol about an inch away from his ear, and waving up and down as though the Trailsman was judging the best way to pretend that the Colt was a hammer and Woods's head was a nail.

Terror gripped his face as he brought up an arm to shield his head from the blow he knew was coming.

"Relax," Fargo said. "I'm in no special hurry. You just finish up what you were doing, and I'll just watch and wait."

Polly thought that was funny, but her paralyzed customer didn't. He just stared up at Fargo, wide-eyed and gape-mouthed, unable to form any words.

"Damn," Fargo said. "I just wanted to talk, and you ain't able to do that, either. You're pitiful, Woods. You can't screw and you can't talk. You're a disappointment to everybody in this room."

The husky man began to disentangle himself from the whore. She pulled some sheets up to cover herself, although she certainly had nothing to hide from either man in the room.

The miner managed to sit up, but still looked befuddled. A minute ago he'd been enjoying Polly's considerable pleasures. Now the man he'd pistol-whipped a week ago was holding a gun next to his head, and smiling like a cat with a canary in its paws.

"So you did go to work for Griswold," Woods finally muttered, while Polly modestly stayed under the sheets as she got a gown around her.

"You're sure confused, Woods."

"Then why're you coming after me?"

"Could have personal reasons. My head's still sore from that little game you played next to the hotel."

"That was all a misunderstanding, Fargo. Let me explain."

"No need for that. I'll do the explaining."

Woods gulped and nodded.

"I'm going to work for you and what's left of the Sedgwicks. I came by to fetch the stuff I've got to take to Denver so you folks can pay off old Griswold."

Woods shook his head. "It won't work. You'll never get there."

"Seems to me that's my worry."

"Not if you're carrying my gold. You'll get caught in a slide or blown off a cliff. Some lucky bastard will find your corpse next spring, and he'll have my gold then. No sirree, Fargo. Jim's idea made sense before the weather turned sour. But nothing's moving across the mountains now, and nothing may move until spring."

"What's going to happen to your claim if you don't pay Griswold?"

"Maybe I've found everything in it worth finding. Plumb amazing to come up with that wire gold in what sure looked like a silver strike."

"Maybe you'd like to see what you could find in Boot Hill."

Woods froze again and then realized he was sitting bare-ass naked. A blush spread over his muscled body as he grabbed a sheet and got as decent as he could.

"Look, Woods, I get where I'm going. And I'm going to Denver with that gold. And you're going to pay me for my trouble. And I leave in the morning."

The miner stared at Fargo. "And you're not working for Griswold?"

"I said I was working for you."

Woods digested the idea. "It would sure simplify life if you did get that gold to Denver. Jesus, I'm tired of the way things have been going."

"So am I."

Two hours later, when Woods had returned from wherever he had cached his forty-pound bonanza, even Fargo gasped at its beauty, and Polly just sat speechless and admired it.

Twined around chunks of smoky quartz, the gold seemed to glow, even under the dim coal-oil lamp. Coils branched into fine stems and delicate little plates that resembled leaves. It looked as though an exuberant vine had been touched by King Midas. There was always talk of wire gold and its radiance, but this was the first time the Trailsman had ever seen such a sample, let alone held it.

"Take good care of it, Fargo," Woods said sadly. He looked like a man who was losing a son.

Before Fargo could assure Woods that his baby was in good hands, the kitchen window shattered as a bullet plowed into the far wall. Rolling back from the table, Fargo pulled the lamp with him and blew it out before stretching out on the floor.

"Damn it," Woods muttered. "I should have known Griswold would try to stop you."

"What makes you so sure it's Griswold?" Fargo whispered back, just as soon as another round finished crossing the room.

"Well, it ain't him exactly. It's that gun he finally hired. That bastard has the only other Henry hereabouts, and I know that sound."

"Stands to reason," Fargo conceded, wondering why folks were so busy fighting each other around here. Nature gave them plenty to fight against—the thin air that made breathing so difficult, the miserable cold climate, the lightning storms of summer, and the frostbite of winter. But they insisted on fighting each other all the time, too.

"Hey, Fargo!" came the shout from outside. "You still in there?"

"Where the hell else would I be?" the Trailsman hollered back as he crawled over to the window and rose to a crouch, hoping like hell that he wouldn't slash himself with any more busted glass. This was getting tiresome.

"Good. I found you. Can you come down to the hotel? Man wants to talk to you there about a job."

"Tell him to go piss up a rope," Fargo replied. "I've got a job."

"It won't hurt you none to listen." The click of another shell being chambered ended the sentence, so the voice in the snow wasn't more than a few yards off.

"I'm listenin' now." Fargo had his pistol ready. "You got my attention."

There was a muffled laugh. "Just drop by the hotel this evening. My boss needs you."

"He needs somebody with brains instead of sawdust."

"That's as may be. I done my job." The voice retreated.

Once they had the lamp lit and some pasteboard stuck in to replace the window pane, Woods glowered at Fargo. "You ain't gonna do that, are you?"

"Do what?"

"You know goddamn well what I'm talking about, Fargo. You're gonna take my gold and cut some deal with Griswold, and I'm gonna be left out in the cold."

"You're indoors and warm enough right now."

"Can't you quit talking in riddles?" The miner kept clenching and unclenching his fists, trying to keep his temper under control before he did something stupid that he might not live long enough to regret.

"See here, Woods. You shot at me the first time I

118

met you. The next time, I caught a pistol butt with my ear. I am trying to save your worthless ass, not because I give a plugged nickel in hell about you, but because there are some half-decent folks you said you'd help. I don't care if you like them just because they hate Griswold, too."

"But I thought you was on our side now."

"Hear me clear. The only side I'm on is mine. I will get your goddamn gold to Denver and get it sold for a good price. You'll keep your claim so you can find more gold or silver or whatever in it. The folks down at the S Bar C can keep their ranch so they can pay you back, or they can sell it with a clear title and you'll get your money. That's your worry, not mine. And what I might or might not say to Rufus Griswold is my worry, not yours. Got that?"

Woods fidgeted some as the notion of protesting died hard under the merciless glare from Fargo's lake-blue eyes.

"Okay," he finally said. "I got the message." He shrugged. "Good luck."

"I'll need that." With the forty pounds of wire gold tucked inside his coat, Fargo didn't exactly step lightly to the hotel. But he got through the snow to the back door of the kitchen, where he let himself in.

The cook didn't seem to be all that bothered when he saw a big man with a gun in his kitchen. That was likely because Fargo had his pistol aimed elsewhere—at the head of the gent lounging against one side of the doorway that led out to the dining room. With a Henry cradled in his arms, he was watching the front door pretty hard.

But he turned when Fargo's first bullet crashed into the doorpost an inch above his head. Even though he had splinters in his scalp to go with the sawdust between his ears, the fellow's instincts were decent as he dropped and started to shoulder the Henry.

Fargo's second bullet nicked one of the man's jug ears before plowing into the wall. "Got your attention?" the Trailsman asked.

The man nodded, shaking droplets of blood from his ear.

"You learn any manners yet? Or do you need some more lessons?"

The gunman's head shook.

Fargo walked past the crouching man, on into the dining room. Gunplay was fairly common in Oro City, judging by how no one looked all that surprised to see him stroll in with a smoking pistol. But on the other hand, they had all stopped eating and talking to look up at him. And the front door didn't close quite so fast that Fargo didn't catch a rear glimpse of some women-folk hurrying out into the cold.

"Nobody's hurt enough to matter," Fargo announced. "If you don't believe me, just ask Jug Ears back there." Fargo spied Griswold, sitting at a table that offered a good view of the door while allowing him to keep his back against the wall. "Evenin'. Your errand boy said you wanted to talk."

"He said he had trouble finding you." Griswold motioned for Fargo to be seated.

"He's going to have more trouble if he doesn't learn that it's generally easier to knock on a door than to start shooting through windows."

Griswold sighed. "It's more or less your own fault, Mr. Fargo."

"How would that be?"

"I wanted to hire you for the job. And you wouldn't take it. It's hard to find good help these days." He slid the bottle over toward Fargo.

The Trailsman poured a shot before replying. "Oh, if you needed a bully, you probably found one. The way he waves his Henry around likely scares most folks into paying you on time."

Griswold laughed. "Actually, I hired him as a body-guard. You'd be surprised how many people hate me."

"No, I don't think I'd be surprised," Fargo said. "And I'm going to be one of them if you don't explain why you sent that halfwit to find me."

For whatever reasons, Griswold was convinced that just about everybody in Oro City hated him and was planning to ruin him. They were spreading nasty ru-mors about his bank being close to insolvency.

Most folks in mining camps trusted a coffee can

120

buried in the backyard a lot more than they trusted banks, anyway. Such talk tended to make people nervous about any money they had deposited in the local bank.

So they'd line up to withdraw their funds. When enough people got in line to demand their money, it was known as a run on the bank. It usually meant the end of the bank.

"Most people just don't understand how banks work," Griswold explained as he offered Fargo a cigar. The Trailsman refused it with thanks. With a penknife, the banker cut off the tip and got the thing burning before continuing.

"They bring in their money, and they seem to think that we've got a bunch of slots in the vault, and we put their money into one of the slots to keep it safe until they withdraw their funds. But we'd never stay in business that way."

"Of course not," Fargo agreed through the cloud of blue smoke. "You lend out most of what you take in, and you just keep enough cash around to handle the daily chores."

The banker nodded. "So we never have enough cash to pay off all the depositors at once. I've tried to manage this bank prudently to make sure that all our loans are performing. I've moved quickly when any of our loans looked shaky. But still people mistrust my bank. There will be a run on it any day."

Fargo had seen bank runs. They were ugly sights, and he was glad he was leaving town, even if he was leaving by wading through four feet of snow up to the highest pass in the Rocky Mountains.

"The only way you stop a run," Griswold said, "is to smile while you pay everybody off. And to have so much gold piled up inside that people just look at it and know that you're solid. Banks are like churches. They run on faith. Except preachers get it easier than we do. Every now and again, our customers demand to see something real."

"Mr. Griswold, I already knew that much about banks. Do you or don't you have anything to say to me?"

The dapper banker sighed and shook his head. "Sorry. Didn't mean to ramble on." He shifted before continuing. "Certainly I have a proposition for you."

Fargo drained his shot and refilled it, and still had to wait some before Griswold got around to business.

"There's ample money at my bank in Buckskin Joe to cover any conceivable run on this bank. All you have to do is get it from there to here, in less than a week. You'll be paid most handsomely."

11

Fargo smiled and looked at Griswold for a moment, amused at the way the local fortune seemed to depend on his crossing the pass.

"Here to there is already on my way. But I'm going to Denver, and I don't figure to make my return in less than a week, unless I sprout wings."

"Mr. Fargo, last week you told me you were on your way to Texas for the winter, and you're still here. You'll change your plans for other people. Why not for me?"

"For one thing, they're mighty disappointed over in Buckskin that they didn't get to hang me the last time I didn't rob your bank there."

Griswold looked perplexed before realization swept across his anxious face. "That robbery attempt. Yes. Three men died there, didn't they?"

"Three men that were trying to rob your bank there to pay your bank here."

"I had a lien on that property."

"I'm sure you did. But those three men died with my bullets in them, and I'm still not sure I did the right thing."

Griswold sank back. "So that was you that stopped the robbery. And no doubt you that broke out of jail with the survivor, poor Jim Sedgwick. It didn't sound right, the way I heard it. I knew there had to be more to the story." As he mulled things over, the banker chewed on the half-done cigar more than he smoked it.

"Damn." The banker repeated it several more times. "And there's four feet of snow here and God knows how much on the pass. And there's a noose waiting for you in Buckskin if you could get there. And no guarantee that you could get back. And you've got another job that's going to take you on east to Denver anyway, if you can get over Mosquito Pass. And you can't take a horse over it, and there's only so much you could carry, anyway."

"There might be a few more problems, but I think you've hit the high spots there." Fargo reached to pour himself another shot and thought better of the idea. "If I had any sense, I'd just get good and drunk and stay here all winter. But I want my horse back."

Griswold looked confused again and decided he'd never get everything sorted out. He straightened. "Then I'm up shit river without a paddle."

"You've got plenty of company."

"Small consolation. You'd do well for yourself, quite well, if you could save this bank."

The room felt stifling. Part of it was the heavy coat that Fargo didn't dare take off, since the huge chunk of gold was tucked inside. Fargo stood. "If I find a way to help you out, I'll let you know. But don't hold your breath."

Griswold just exhaled as Fargo went to see about a room.

Its sheet-metal stove glowed red when Fargo trimmed the lamp and nodded off to sleep after checking his gear. Even so, he had to break ice in the pitcher when he rose before sunrise. And that seemed downright warm, almost tropical, compared to bitterness outside under the sparkling sky.

The way the packed snow crunched and squeaked under his feet at the edge of Oro City, it had to be at least twenty below. For late October, that was goddamn cold, even for the mountains. But you could always expect some mean temperatures when the sky was clear after a big storm. Clouds held in such warmth as there might be. Once they blew off, the air could get brutal.

But it wasn't all that bad, so long as Fargo took his time so that he never gasped in air through his mouth. Take air in through your nose, and it gets a chance to warm up before it gets down into your chest. Gulp it in, and you get cold clear inside and out.

There wasn't any wind, which would have made travel totally impossible. For a considerable distance up the gulch, Fargo was able to walk on a packed trail, since men were still trying to go back and forth to their claims, trying to get everything they could before admitting that it was finally winter and time to do something else.

From the last working claim to timberline, though, sustained movement was mostly a matter of chance. In spots, the sun had managed to melt enough of the top layer of snow to crust it. But only in spots. Everywhere else, Fargo's boots sank, and sank, and sank, past his knees, past his thighs, sometimes past his waist. Climbing out of those self-made holes was exhausting. It was also exasperating as hell to get out of one, take two steps, and find himself sinking again.

Fargo couldn't find any pattern that would tell him by dim starlight whether the crust was reliable. Fortunately, in only two hours, he managed the mile or so to timberline, where the going got easier.

Much easier. The strong winds had blown in from the west and raced up toward the top of the Mosquito Range. Up here, there were no trees to slow the wind and make it drop its burden of snow. Even the snow that should have fallen here had been scooped up by the wind and carried on—maybe to Kansas, the way that wind had been howling.

Wherever the snow had gone, Fargo was glad it wasn't under him. It was enough that he had a steep climb among loose rocks in subzero weather while trying to manage with a heavy canvas pack on his back and his Sharps carbine slung over his shoulder—while he still felt light-headed and got tired more easily than he should. Maybe he was so light-headed that he couldn't think things through, and that's how he'd ended up agreeing to do this job, even when he'd had to argue some to take it on. Damn little was making sense. The only thing to think about was putting one foot in front of the other.

The mystery of the disappearing snow was solved when Fargo crested the Mosquito Range, getting his first glimpse of the morning sun.

Before him sloped a great billowy expanse. It started in wall-sided cornices that perched along the crest. From there on down to the trees, at least a million miles below him, there was nothing but white. The wind had sailed up the west side with a load of snow. Once over the top, the wind just kept going, but without enough velocity to carry its white burden. The principle was the same as the snow fences people used out on the prairie, but here a huge mountain range served as the fence.

Fargo just stood there and caught his breath for a few minutes. Maybe they had been right, and this was impossible. Even if the rest of the trip was downhill, no way could any man less than twenty feet tall wade through this. The worst of it was that the snow wasn't sitting comfortable.

All around, there were little tracks, straight lines that went down the hillside. Small clumps of snow had broken off from the cornices and started to roll. There was nothing to stop them. Many of them had grown into man-sized snowballs along the way, judging by the size of their tracks.

There wasn't any evidence of a major avalanche yet, but that was just a matter of time.

Fargo stood on the ridge. "Damn." He didn't feel a bit better. "Double damn. Hell. Shit. Fuck." Those shouts finally relieved his tension. But what was he going to do? Go back to Oro City and see if he could stay out of the war that was going to develop? Go forward and get trapped in a snowdrift? Stand here and freeze to death?

The Trailsman's ears caught a groaning, crackling sound, as if the mountains were swearing back at him.

It was coming almost from under his feet, which he'd been stomping even as he stood in order to keep circulation going. The sound, though, came from over to the right about fifty yards. There the wind-piled snow cornice was breaking off as a chasm opened behind it.

Awestruck, Fargo watched. The front wall of the cornice—a mass about fifty feet long and ten feet deep, perhaps thirty feet high—slid down the slope so slowly that it shouldn't have been making any noise, let alone all that groaning.

Teetering, the wall of snow threatened to collapse into a jumbled pile. But then it rocked forward, on down the snow-covered slope.

That was all the encouragement the snowfield needed to head downhill in a hurry. The mass gained momentum, scouring the ground behind it almost clean as it began to race down the mountain with a roar.

Fargo couldn't help holding his breath as he watched the tremendous slide clean the hillside down to timberline. The trees didn't seem to slow it enough to matter; they cracked like matchsticks when the slide front, by now at least thirty feet high, crashed into them with such force that some towering evergreens were thrown into the air.

The thunderlike rumble filled Fargo's ears as his eyes followed the slide's continuing downward swath. When it hit bottom and could go no further, a huge cloud of snow erupted. Seconds later the explosive sound reached his high vantage.

"Guess there was a good reason to stand here a spell," Fargo told himself. Then he asked, "What happens next?" before he realized he'd been looking at the answer.

The slide that he'd set off with his shouts hadn't taken every last flake of snow with it. But what remained in its path couldn't be enough to cause trouble. And there certainly wasn't enough snow remaining there to run again, which meant that if there was a safe way down this mountain, it was the slide path.

Finding a safe way to the slide path might be a problem, since getting there would mean traipsing under a looming cornice for thirty or forty yards. Fargo shouted at it, then heaved a few rocks that way. Just to be sure, he fired his Sharps into the hazard. Not that the bullet would matter to that heap of snow, but the gun's booming report should topple the snow if it was destined to go soon.

The ominous cornice stayed put, although Fargo kept looking up at it while he waded through the hip-deep snow at its foot. Once he got to the slide, he could practically hop and skip to the bottom.

Down where there had been trees not very long ago, Fargo paused to marvel at the desolation. He'd seen what happened to buildings when their steam boilers exploded. Once he'd happened upon the shaft house of a mine just a few minutes after someone got careless with a load of black powder. But the closest thing in memory was a town in Missouri after a tornado had churned through it.

Even that wasn't quite the same. Tornadoes swirled and jumped, leaving a few things standing. This snowslide, a quarter-mile wide by the time it got into the trees, left nothing in its wake—just a wide, clean silence. Fargo followed the broad path ever downward.

It all had to end somewhere. The slide had roared downslope at an angle to the trend of the valley. When it hit the creek bed at the floor, it tried to climb on up the other side. Given that it had to work against the gravity that had provided its force, the slide hadn't done a bad job—its tongue lapped a good two hundred yards up from the creek bed.

That was just a guess, since the creek bed was buried under tons of snow, rocks, trees, and anything else that might have been in the way. The mass was still settling; trees cracked and rocks gnashed to disturb the eerie silence.

No, there was more. Fargo turned toward the soft sound that came from somewhere on the downstream side, off where the trees still stood. He reached inside his greatcoat and got his pistol before heading into the trees. The Utes had more sense about such matters than white folks did and generally cleared out of the mountains before the first good snowfall. But this storm had come on suddenly, so there was a chance that some band hadn't yet moved to one of the warmer low valleys a hundred miles to the west.

Every sense alert, Fargo moved deliberately through the stand of red-barked spruce. Over here, the snow was surprisingly shallow, less than a foot deep. The eastbound storm must have dumped most of its snow on the other side of the range. Up high, this side got what blew over, along with the leavings.

There it was. That sound again. A grunt and a

moan, like someone hurting bad. Fargo edged down-hill for about a hundred yards before he found its source—a man trying to grab an aspen sapling to pull himself up.

Still wary, Fargo studied the surroundings carefully before getting any closer. Only one set of tracks in the snow, and the groaning man didn't look likely to cause trouble.

He was big and broad-shouldered, dressed for a mountain winter. Fargo guessed they were close to the same size, although the struggling man's thick, close-cropped hair showed tinges of gray, as did his beard. The weathered face with the laborious expression indi-cated that its owner was at least a decade older than the Trailsman.

The man didn't seem to notice Fargo's approach. On his knees in the snow, he'd grab the sapling. Then his ungloved hands would lose their grip. Or his knees would buckle. If he managed to get on his feet, they'd slide out from under him.

Feeling disgusted with himself for standing there and watching, Fargo stepped on over. "Need a hand?"

The man turned slowly. "Why, yes, I do."

Fargo got next to him and knelt. No sign of blood or mayhem, but the fellow sure seemed under the weather. The only way they could get him standing was for Fargo to get his left arm across the man's back and under an armpit, while the gent's right arm went across the Trailsman's broad shoulders. Even at that the man was so big, and so unsteady, that it was touch and go for a few moments.

He leaned against Fargo, wheezing and catching his breath, for about a minute before he felt solid enough to speak. "Thank you, my son."

12

"Son? As best I know, we're not related at all," Fargo replied while trying to keep his feet underneath him so that they both didn't topple into the snow. Between the load he'd already been carrying, and the weight now pressing against him, his boots wanted to slide away.

"We are all God's children," the man said, as if that explanation were more than sufficient.

"That's as may be," Fargo conceded. "But let's tend to the here and now. What happened to you?"

The man shook his head. "I-I guess I don't know. Where are we?"

"Not too far from Alma. On the uphill side, toward Mosquito Pass."

The older man's graying beard shook again in confusion. Smaller tremors racked his body; his bare fingers were turning blue and his lips were a pale purple. Wordless, he just clutched the Trailsman.

"Can you manage by yourself for a couple minutes so I can look around?" Fargo asked. If the man couldn't tell him anything, his tracks would.

The man nodded. But he was just being polite, because dread was showing all over him at the thought of being left alone. So Fargo stayed put and scanned the scene carefully, starting at the aspen sapling the man had been trying to grab when he had happened by.

Less than a yard away, the snow looked as though it had been swept in one spot, and some yellow showed there. So the gent had stopped to take a leak here, only a couple hundred yards from the bottom of the snowslide.

Short steps led to the spot. The tracks had to be fresh, although they lacked the sharpness of new tracks. But the avalanche, when it bottomed out with that explosion, had loosed a cloud of powdery snow that still frosted the nearby trees. So that explained the appearance of the tracks.

It also meant that the man had arrived at this spot before the slide hit. He'd been standing there when a mountain of snow started coming his way. No way to tell from there just precisely where it would hit.

"Now what would I do in that circumstance?" Fargo wondered aloud as his companion got a handle on his shivering and started standing straighter. "I'd hear it coming, and I'd want to get out of its way, but who's to say whether you're in its way or not? Maybe you'd run the wrong way if you tried to get away. So I'd grab something and hold on, and hope."

The man hadn't been in the slide's direct path. But the slide had caused a considerable noise when it hit. That, or the stuff that was flying everywhere then, could have knocked this gent out. It must have stunned him so that he had trouble standing up, and even more trouble remembering who he was and where he might be headed.

Fargo was satisfied that he knew what must have happened here, and his keen eyes followed the tracks across a small aspen-rimmed clearing perhaps a dozen yards wide. On the other side, the snow had been trampled some. Beyond that disturbed area, there were tracks, sure enough. But the trail was peculiar, unlike anything in the Trailsman's experience.

Fargo squinted. The trail wasn't footprints, and it wasn't made by snowshoes. It was two parallel grooves in the snow, wending on downhill through the trees toward Alma.

Fearing that he might get as confused as the man he was supporting, Fargo stared intently at the trampled area. Almost invisible in the dark shadows that contrasted with the glaring snow, two boards sat propped against a tree.

Each must have run at least ten feet long, and wasn't more than four or five inches wide. Each had one pointed end that curved, and a leather strap in the middle.

So those must have been what the bartender in Oro City had been talking about when he'd mentioned "Norwegian snowshoes." Their generous length would spread a man's weight over the snow and keep him from sinking in, just as the width of the familiar webbed snowshoes kept one from falling too far into the snow.

The man's recent past was now clear to Fargo. He'd been bound up Mosquito Pass from Alma. He'd stopped to rest, and taken off his Norwegian snowshoes. He'd stretched a little, and gone over to take a leak. The slide hit bottom with a force that addled him.

Once the Trailsman had maneuvered himself and the befuddled man across the clearing, he saw that the boards had been coated with pine tar, to keep water from sinking in. The bottoms also sported a shiny layer of beeswax. That would make them slippery. But a man would have enough trouble staying up on these things even if they weren't slippery.

Their short walk across the clearing hadn't helped the older gent worth mention. He was starting to shiver some more, and he'd need to get warm soon.

Fargo studied on their options. Alma couldn't be more than a couple miles away. But the day was getting on, and there was no telling how awful the trip would be. So it must be time to build a fire and put on some coffee to warm this gent up inside and out. By first light tomorrow, they could be on their way to Alma. Somebody there could figure out what happened next. Fargo had to get to Denver, and this was going to cost him at least a day on what was already a tight schedule.

"Goddamn," he muttered. Before he could turn his attention to gathering firewood, the older gent complained.

"Do not take the Lord's name in vain, young man," he rasped.

"Sorry," Fargo apologized, annoyed by the man's sanctimonious attitude, yet pleased that his companion seemed at least somewhat aware of the visible world.

Next to the boardlike snowshoes was a long, crude

staff, also leaning against the tree. It must help with balance when somebody was teetering on those boards, Fargo decided. But it also worked just fine for probing down to see how deep the snow was here—about two feet. No need, then, to lay a bed of boughs and try to build a fire atop the snow.

Pawing at the snow like a dog, the Trailsman quickly dug a yard-wide crater down to the ground. Within minutes, he filled it with dead branches snapped off nearby spruce. The flames felt welcome, but Fargo did not allow himself to rest. Night was coming on. He dare not let the fire go out, and there were more pleasant things to do in the dark than scramble after firewood.

Not that this night was going to be one of those pleasant ones. The cloudless sky meant that the temperature would plunge once the sun set, which would be any minute now. Given a thick bedroll and a warm woman, even that would be tolerable. But this night would be spent with a light bedroll—just a couple of blankets—and a shivering man who looked utterly doleful.

Fargo pulled a tin can out of his pack and worked the lid off with his belt knife. Stewed tomatoes weren't his favorite trail food, but the hotel's meager pantry hadn't given him much choice. Once the can was perched in the fire, he checked on his companion.

The befuddled man wasn't totally witless. He'd pulled down his long snowshoes and laid them to make a seat next to the fire. Fargo sat down next to him and felt more encouraged. The gent had stuck his hands in his pockets and found some thick woolen mittens which he was now pulling on.

"You feeling any better?" Fargo asked as he bent down to fetch the warming tomatoes.

"I believe so," the man answered. "It's starting to come back to me." His shaking hands took the tin from Fargo, and he took a healthy swig of mushy vegetables and their juice. "That's quite warming."

"Sorry I don't have any whiskey," Fargo said. Before he could get a good mouthful, his companion started shouting.

"Whiskey! That's the Devil's potion. It's poison, that's what it is. It's a cruel thief. Whiskey steals the wits of men and the virtue of women."

"Then I'm not sorry that I don't have any whiskey with me," Fargo rejoined. "You have any idea who you are or where you're from or what you do?"

The man mulled for a short spell, then clasped his hands under his beard, closed his deep-set brown eyes, and bowed his head. During this silent prayer, Fargo stared and tried to get his own answers.

His companion was certainly a devout man. He'd objected to Fargo's swearing, and he had no use for liquor. And now he was praying for answers.

Which meant he could be a preacher, but that didn't quite add up. Preachers favored broadcloth, not ragged frontier gear. They also favored staying indoors. And if one of them had to go somewhere, he'd take the stage. He wouldn't be traipsing around the mountains with a couple of bent boards strapped to his feet. Further, most parsons Fargo had encountered had been frail, bookish sorts; this fellow was muscular and husky, with a weathered face.

When the man's brown eyes met Fargo's lake-blue stare, he apologized. "Please forgive me, stranger."

"I can't think of anything you've done that would call for an apology."

"Young man, I have delayed your journey."

"Those things happen," the Trailsman responded while heaving some more branches into the fire. "I'll get you somewhere comfortable tomorrow, and then I'll head on."

"I would be most grateful," the man intoned. "But my mission is to go to Oro City."

At least the gent was talking about something real, so Fargo pushed him. "What's in Oro City?"

"Perhaps my livelihood," the man responded. "The miners here seem unwilling to support a ministry, yet this is where the need for the Gospel is greatest."

The man *was* a preacher. And maybe he was starting to remember some simple facts. "Who are you?" Fargo asked. "Can you remember your name, yet?"

The man nodded and smiled. "It's all coming to me

now." He paused and bowed his head momentarily, then stuck out a mittened hand to shake. "John L. Dyer."

Fargo shook his hand and searched his memory. "You'd be Father Dyer, the Methodist missionary?"

Dyer nodded. "And who would you be?"

"Skye Fargo."

Dyer leaned back a bit, then straightened. "I have heard of you." His words were coming slow, but the man was starting to regain his full intellect. "You're the Trailsman." Then he chuckled.

"Something funny about that, parson?" Fargo asked.

"Not really," Dyer conceded. "It's just that if the Lord had to deliver me into anyone's hands in this condition, He couldn't have picked a better pair of hands—judging by reputation, anyway. I cannot recall ever meeting you before."

"That's flattersome, reverend." Fargo passed the boiling tomatoes. "No, I don't think our paths have crossed. If I'd seen you before, I'd have known who you were. I'd just heard of you. Any man that makes his rounds to the mining camps and thunders against greed, drunkenness, dancing, cardplaying, gambling, and fornication is going to end up getting talked about plenty, even if most folks don't pay much mind to the message."

"Your mission is to find the right path on this world," Dyer responded. "Mine is to put people on the right path to the next."

"Glad to hear we've got something in common, reverend."

"Just call me John, Skye."

"Okay, John. Way I read sign, you headed out of Alma this morning on your Norwegian snowshoes. You stopped to stretch some without those boards on your feet and to relieve yourself. Then that slide came roaring down and gave you some sort of concussion that you're coming out of now."

The flickering light revealed Dyer's nod, so Fargo continued. "Why was it so important to get to Oro City? Mosquito Pass is no joy in the summer, let alone now that winter's settling in. And it fixes to get a lot worse."

"It's a long story, Skye."

"We've got all night. Look on it as a blessing. You've got an audience that doesn't dare fall asleep."

Dyer, who'd been a lumberjack in Wisconsin before feeling the call of the ministry, had been assigned by the Methodist authorities to carry the Word to the sin-filled mining camps that dotted the highest section of the Rocky Mountains.

His circuit included Oro City, Buckskin Joe, Alma, Fairplay, Tarryall, Breckenridge, Montgomery, Hamilton, and half a dozen other little settlements that were damn near impossible to reach without wings. None of them could boast a real church building, so Father Dyer preached out of saloons and private homes, sometimes even outdoors.

Even if some of those camps were prospering, they weren't real generous about supporting the preacher when he passed the hat.

"Just last summer," Dyer recounted, "the bishop summoned me to Denver, and I had to walk because I didn't have the stage fare."

"How was the walk?" Fargo noticed that Dyer had emptied the tomato can, so he packed it with snow and stuck it back into the fire. "I'm curious because that's what I've got ahead of me."

"Long," Dyer said. "But not unpleasant. If you have the means, though, the stage is still running from Tarryall to Denver."

Fargo turned so that he could warm a different part of his body. "John, why were you headed up Mosquito Pass this morning? Nobody crosses that thing in the winter. It's bad enough in the summer."

"That's what the last mail contractor said. But I believe it can be done. Didn't you just come across it?"

"It isn't something I'd go out of my way to do, John. And what's this about mail contractors?"

"If I have to make these rounds anyway, I could carry the mail. That income would sustain my ministry. I believe that if I can demonstrate that I can cross the pass, even after a big snowfall, then I might receive the contract to carry the mail."

"And those boards, or Norwegian snowshoes, or whatever you call them, will let you get around the mountains in the winter?"

"Certainly," Dyer replied. "I learned the art in Wisconsin. Out here, they call them Norwegian snowshoes, but back there, they call them 'skis.' And when they go out on the boards, they go 'skiing.' "

"Looks to me like they'd be troublesome, a lot more trouble than regular webs." Fargo reached down with his gloved hand and rubbed it along the waxed surface they were sitting on. "You've got these slicked up," the Trailsman observed, "so I don't know how you'd go up any kind of hill, even a gentle one, unless you sidestepped, which would be tiresome. Going down, you could end up sliding so fast that you'd plow right into a tree, or maybe sail off a cliff. On the flat, or standing still, balance could be tricky. Most of us don't know how to walk in boots that're ten feet long."

Dyer's shaggy head nodded and he broke out into a toothy smile. "I worried about all that, the first time I tried skiing. But somehow it all works, Skye. You saw the tracks I made coming up here. That's up a grade. Did I sidestep?"

"Not that I noticed," Fargo admitted.

"If you wax the bottoms right and you are mindful of how you step, you can shuffle right up most hills. If the hill gets so steep that you begin to backslide, you can make a V with your skis."

"Leave a track like a herringbone."

"I suppose it would. At first I crossed the skis with almost every step I took, and I stumbled and fell often. But one learns to keep his feet straight. The pole I carry helps with balance. Sometimes I do go too fast downhill and fear that I cannot steer the skis. So then I just fall down."

"Reckon that would stop you." Fargo threw some more snow into the can and reached for a few more sticks. "Say, John, what's it feel like to shoot down a hill when you're on your skis?"

Dyer laughed from the depths of his big frame. "It

is so thrilling, so joyful, Skye, that I am beginning to suspect that if skiing on the Sabbath is not a sin, then it ought to be."

That brought the conversation around to topics which Dyer obviously preferred. Certainly the man had to talk about something if they were going to be stuck here, awake all night. And men did like to talk about their work. But this figured to get tedious, or worse.

The long explanation of the fires of Hell just reminded Fargo how comfortable the place would have to be, at least in comparison to the freezing air that enveloped the mountains. Such warmth and cheer as their little fire provided was hardly adequate.

But maybe it was just as well that Hell sounded so good tonight. For Fargo was certainly bound there. Dyer assured the Trailsman that everything he enjoyed was sinful.

A comforting shot of warm, smooth whiskey. Shooting back at anybody stupid enough to fire at you. An interesting, if not always profitable, evening of poker. Whirling and stomping at a county hoe-down—why, even that music was wicked. And a night in a woman's arms, fornicating furiously and acting lecherous and lascivious every time the mood struck.

The more sins Dyer denounced, the more wistful Fargo felt. It was bad enough to be stuck here out in the cold. But did the preacher have to keep reminding Fargo of all the earthly pleasures he was missing?

Arguing, or even answering the minister's challenges, would be a waste of energy. Fargo got through the night just by listening and saying "uh huh," every now and again. By the time the sky started to pale and the fainter stars began to vanish, Dyer was pretty well wound down.

"Skye, would you join me in a prayer?"

"I'll bow my head and I won't interrupt. That's about the best I can do, John."

"Oh, Lord," Dyer implored, "please hear the plea of your humble and unworthy servant. Accept his gratitude for sending this stranger, who succored your servant unquestioningly, just as our Lord Jesus instructed in the parable of the Good Samaritan. If it be thy will, Lord, allow your servant to continue his ministry here where the fields are whitened for the harvest. And if it be thy will, Lord, redeem this stranger who has helped your servant; bring him to the fold that he may experience the power and glory of a life of virtue. In the name of the Father, and the Son, and the Holy Spirit, amen."

Dyer turned to Fargo. "I'll be praying for your soul, Skye."

"That's considerate of you," the Trailsman admitted, but he sure hoped Dyer's prayers for his virtue weren't successful. "I mean that. But we'd best worry about this world right now, rather than the next."

"How so?" The preacher rose and started picking up.

"You got stunned yesterday. Parts of you were pretty cold when I happened along. You'd best get somewhere warm where you can rest up, take a hot bath or whatever, for a few days until you can be sure you're all in one piece."

"But I must get to Oro City."

"They aren't getting any mail now," the Trailsman proclaimed. "It'll still be there whenever you decide to try skiing this pass—if a slide doesn't get you."

Dyer nodded. "Perhaps that is for the best. The Lord sent you, the Trailsman, to me, and I'd best accept that guidance."

"Doubt that my instructions came from that high, John. I was just on my way somewhere."

"The Lord works in mysterious ways, Skye. And you might be one of them."

13

It wasn't even really day yet when the two men struck out. The snow sported something of a crust which, except for one step out of every fifty or so, was thick enough to support both men. They made fair progress through the trees, even though Dyer often snagged overhead branches with the skis he was carrying over his shoulder.

By the time the sky turned pink, they could see Alma slumbering below them—fifty or sixty buildings of assorted sizes, smoke drifting out of most chimneys. A few hardy souls stirred along its main street, and the horses over at the livery stable corral sent up a cloud of fog.

"You have your parsonage there?" Fargo asked.

"Parsonage?" Dyer replied. "Such as it is. It's a one-room log cabin with a hide for a door. And it's over in Buckskin Joe."

"Think I know it. By Silver Heels's place, isn't it?" The Trailsman instantly regretted bringing up a dancer's name.

"That woman may otherwise live a life of virtue, for all I know. But her performances inspire wicked thoughts, even in men who try to remain steadfast."

Fargo didn't see fit to improve Dyer's knowledge about what Silver Heels did offstage. Better to change the subject, anyway.

"Say, John, think I could try getting from here to town on those skis of yours?"

"You'll likely fall down."

"And I'll likely get up again and keep trying. The way you talked about it, it's something I ought to know how to do—no telling when it might come in handy. And the only way I learn anything is by doing it."

Dyer seemed agreeable and laid the skis down. Fargo tugged at the buckles on the leather straps until his boots seemed secure. Standing up, he took several sliding steps. That was easy enough. He took another step and tried to turn. The ski tips crossed and he found himself in the snow, falling with such force that he broke through the crust. Dyer walked over and gave him a hand.

"I warned you it wouldn't be easy. Especially without the pole. I think we burned it."

"Could be. Got any suggestions?"

They both looked around; their eyes landed simultaneously on a puny aspen stand several yards off.

"None of those is big enough to make a pole," Dyer noted.

Fargo shuffled over and bent down with his knife. "I'll try this with two little poles, one in each hand."

"Never saw that," Dyer said. "Everybody skis with just one big pole. But you're the one risking your neck."

"It'll be good, clean fun," Fargo answered. "Meet you in town?"

"I'll be there to pick up the pieces." Dyer started walking down the flank of the hill, taking a roundabout way toward town. Fargo moved gingerly, just a bit at a time, to get his feet around so that he was pointed downhill, toward town.

That hill hadn't looked all that steep before. But now it looked steeper than the side of a cow's face. Both scraggly trees that poked out of the snow grew to immense proportions, with limbs that could reach out and club a sliding man from yards away. Once a man got going, he might never stop. The hill bottomed out right at Alma's main street, but that was merely a level stretch. After that, the terrain continued to drop. Besides, there were folks in the street now.

Fargo closed his eyes to keep common sense from overwhelming him. Pushing both poles downward, he shoved forward. Moments later, he opened his eyes. An exhilarating rush of air hit his face, and the countryside was speeding by. Then he became part of the countryside.

It happened so fast that Fargo wasn't sure what he'd done wrong. One instant, he felt like he had wings, and the next instant, he was buried face first on a snowy hillside, spread-eagled with his ankles bent to peculiar and painful angles.

Getting straightened out took an awful amount of twisting and wiggling. Getting up was even worse. Every time he moved, he sank deeper into the snow. He couldn't stick his arm down to push himself up, because then his arm would plunge down halfway to China. The Trailsman studied on his predicament for a few moments.

Concentrated weight sank through the snow. Spread-out weight stayed atop it. How to spread the force of his arm? Get both saplings into one hand. Make an X shape, and grab it in the middle.

Fargo got to his feet and checked to make sure he hadn't lost anything. The canvas pack still tugged at his back, so the hefty chunk of wire gold hadn't gone anywhere. The shoulder-slung Sharps had shifted some, and its barrel was packed with snow. Just to be sure, he unbuttoned his coat and checked his Colt. Amazing how snow could creep up everywhere when a man fell in it—even into a holstered pistol. But there wasn't much sense in drying out the weapons, since he'd likely fall again and fill them with snow before he got to Alma.

Fargo shifted slightly before realizing that his skis were still pointed downhill. With a muffled hiss, he was moving again. Moving damn fast. Lean back and enjoy it, maybe. That seemed to work.

But this was like being on a runaway horse. No control at all. What had Dyer said? To fall down. Never mind. That was happening enough on its own, without any conscious effort. The surroundings slowed, then dissolved into a haze of powdery whiteness.

At any rate, getting back up was much easier this time around, now that there was some method to it.

Moving downhill again, Fargo inadvertently pointed his toes toward each other. The skis responded, their tips almost touching as their backs flared out. His pace slowed to something almost controllable, especially when he flexed his ankles inward. There was sure a lot to consider here, though. The tips crossed and Fargo went flying forward again.

When Fargo pulled himself out of the snow this time, he pointed the skis off to the side. They were still headed downhill, but not straight downhill. The open hillside provided ample room for a traverse, but all good things come to an end. And the end of the hillside was a stand of vicious-looking lodgepole.

Working instinctively, because he sure didn't know what he was doing, Fargo shifted his feet and balance, leaning some on his poles in the process. When he caught his bearings, he'd pretty much reversed his direction. He was traversing the hill going the other way.

No wonder Father Dyer had said this might be too much fun to do on a Sunday. Grinning like a fox in a henhouse, the Trailsman looked down on Alma, which was getting closer by the second. It was hard to tell if Dyer had made it down there yet. At least a dozen bundled-up people stood in the street, watching Fargo's performance on the hillside.

They got a good laugh a few moments later. Too busy looking toward town, he hadn't noticed a dip in the snow. His skis went down the dip just fine, but he hadn't leaned back to pull up the tips when they started out of the dip. The skis went straight into the rising snow and stopped. Fargo fell face forward before he stopped.

This one hurt as Fargo's nose slammed into a ski. Somewhere in the process, he also managed to fill one ear with snow, and clawing fingers of cold now probed at his innards. The Trailsman got up and shook himself, then pulled off a glove and dug the snow out of his ear.

It quit throbbing and he started back down. Maybe this wasn't quite as much fun as it'd seemed a couple moments ago, but still, it beat hell out of wading through drifts. Even if none of Father Dyer's preaching seemed likely to stick, Fargo did owe the man for explaining how this was done.

The next time he fell, he was no more than a stone's throw from the edge of Alma, where the crowd of onlookers had doubled or more. Determined to get to town without another tumble, Fargo clambered up.

He didn't know the man that hollered at him. But he could sure hear what he was shouting.

"Hey, you. Stop where you are!"

"What's your problem? You own this snow?"

The man pulled up a pistol, which explained why the crowd started edging back. "You're a wanted man," he explained, "and you're under arrest."

"What'd I do?"

"You son of a bitch, you know goddamn well what you did. And you're not gonna get away with it."

The medium-height man with the sandy beard and the pointed gun was likely on the lean side, although his heavy coat gave him some bulk. No star was showing, but he sure stood there with the assurance of a confident lawman. He didn't look familiar at all, but there was no telling who might have looked in on the Buckskin jail during Fargo's generally unconscious stay.

The onlookers had pretty well cleared the street now. Those who remained stood close by the storefronts, and Father Dyer was now among them.

"Just tell me what I did," Fargo said, bringing up his poles as he lifted his hands.

"You ain't gonna get away with robbin' the bank over in Buckskin and then bustin' out of jail and killin' ol' Pete Green an' burnin' up the sheriff's office. You can come along peaceable so as we can string you up, or you can die right there were you stand, on top of them snowshoes. Entirely up to you."

The deputy's head turned, but his gun didn't, at a shout from the side.

"That man is no robber or murderer," Father Dyer boomed. "He saved my life yesterday."

"Stay out of this, preacher. You don't know what he's done."

Dyer stepped toward the deputy. "I'll not stand here and see an innocent man shot down in cold blood." The preacher's big arms and ham-sized fists were up.

"Wait, John," Fargo shouted. "Everybody hold up. I'll come on down."

If they heard him, it didn't register. Dyer kept taking big steps toward the deputy. When he got within reach, the lawman's free arm swung round, the windmill motion catching the surprised Dyer square in the face.

Before the preacher finished hitting the ground, Fargo was on his way. He shoved his poles in as far ahead as he could and pulled like a man rowing against the current. The poles stayed behind as Fargo shot forward, straight down the hill toward Alma's main street.

Struggling to keep his balance, Fargo flexed his knees. More control that way. He shifted his butt back and his head down. Couldn't see a whole lot that way, even when he lifted his eyes and caught a faceful of powder. But he was traveling straight and fast. For the first time all day, he felt secure atop the skis, not like he was teetering and about to tumble any second.

By the time the deputy looked up from Dyer's efforts to regain his feet, Fargo was only a few yards away, and coming straight at him.

The lawman stared, slack-jawed, and started to bring up his pistol. "What the—" Anything else he might have had to say got cut off.

The skis struck first, slicing the footing right out from under the deputy. He rolled back, tottering, which left his belly wide open. Fargo charged head first, ramming the man's chest.

They both went down in a heap, landing almost silently on the hard-packed street snow. Unable to move much, since the skis were still on his boots, Fargo grabbed at whatever was handy, and twisted.

That was the deputy's free arm, and the bastard was trying to come around with his other hand. Despite the force of their collision, he'd managed to hold onto the gun. Fargo gave the hammerlock a savage turn. The pain registered on the winded deputy's face, but he was still fixing to use the gun.

Bringing a knee up to where it would do the most good didn't work. Not that Fargo didn't try. But from the waist down, he was useless, the way that his legs and feet and skis were all snarled together. Something else might be tugging down there.

Fargo didn't have time to look, though. The trick was to keep from getting pistol-whipped or shot. Rocking on the pack, Fargo used the motion for leverage. His fist slammed into the deputy's beard. The man's head snapped back, but he managed to shake Fargo's hammerlock.

The Trailsman was on his back and the deputy, now starting to sit up, was astride him. Fargo bucked and pitched and tried to grab the man's head, to keep him close. Any distance, any distance at all, and the lawman would be able to use that pistol.

With a tremendous groaning effort, the lithe deputy pulled his torso back and up, despite Fargo's grip. The Trailsman's hands started to slide off the man's shoulders, and Fargo reached for the bastard's scrawny neck. There had to be some way to stop this maniac.

That likely would have been the way, but Fargo never did learn for sure. Father Dyer, sprawled on the ground by Fargo's tangled feet, had managed to pull one ski off. He got up and swung the thing, taking aim at the back of the deputy's head.

Since the preacher had once been a lumberjack, he knew how to swing an ax. His aim was true, and his arms retained their strength. With a sickening splat, the edge of the ski caught the deputy's neck. Fargo didn't see that, but he felt the transmitted force of the blow. The lawman sagged forward. In an instant, Fargo had the gun and was shoving the weight off him.

Returning a favor, Dyer helped him to his feet.

"Thanks, John," Fargo said, then just stood there, catching his breath. "I don't know how much longer that would have lasted if you hadn't stepped in. You really caught him good upside the head."

Dyer pointed down to the ski. "Not all that hard. Didn't even break it."

Fargo shoved the gun into a coat pocket and looked around. Except for the knocked-out deputy, the street was empty. The disarmed lawman lay sprawled out on his side in the snow. A bit of blood seeped out the back of his neck, but he was still breathing.

There were still folks watching from the side, and Fargo didn't know enough local politics to know which side they might be on. If they didn't care for the local law, he'd be a hero. If they did, there'd be a damn lynch mob after him.

Dyer came through Alma fairly often, though, and he'd already made up his mind. "Skye, you'd best move on." The preacher's head shook and he shut his eyes. His legs trembled a bit. He was still suffering from that concussion, and the deputy's swing hadn't helped a bit.

"What's the matter?"

"Just feel light-headed, that's all."

"Then we'll get you home to your cabin in Buckskin Joe."

"But you're not safe anywhere in Park County."

As if to emphasize that, some of the bystanders built up their courage. One hollered something mean to Fargo, and two others were fetching guns from under their coats.

The deputy's gun likely didn't shoot the same way Fargo's Colt did, so the Trailsman shot wider than he otherwise might have. Even so, the bullet that slammed into the stable wall behind one man's head came close enough to make the fellow thoughtful.

Fargo surveyed the audience. All had clustered along one side of the street, the sunny side, where they'd be a little warmer than otherwise. There were eight men of all sizes, but only two looked likely to do anything. And one of them already had splinters in his ear.

Looking straight at the other one, a husky gent who had to work at the stable, given that he was standing in its doorway and didn't have a coat on, Fargo explained what was going to happen.

"You're going to rent Father Dyer and me a wagon. He's feeling kind of sickly, and I'm going to get him home." Fargo turned his eyes to the others. "You're going to get your deputy inside and see what can be done for him. Father Dyer's no murderer, so if that bastard doesn't pull through, the blood is on your hands."

Dyer looked ashen at the thought that he might

have taken a life, but there was a satisfying scurry of onlookers. Except for the jasper in the stable door.

"You can't go nowhere in a wagon, mister."

"Then rig us up something."

"Horses?"

That sounded reasonable, being as the roads were packed down pretty solid. But Fargo had been through these woozy-headed feelings himself. Better to be sure that Dyer got home, and there weren't any guarantees that the preacher wouldn't just fall out of a saddle.

"Well?" the surly stablehand hollered.

"Something besides horses. You got a sleigh?"

As it turned out, they did have a sleigh. A pretty fancy one, at that, with rolled and tucked leather upholstery and a canvas tonneau. It came with a matched pair of high-stepping bays whose calked shoes would provide good traction.

Best of all, it was already hitched up, ready for a run down to the stage station at Tarryall. The hostler complained about Fargo's manners in just up and taking it. Fargo reached for some coins and offered to pay. Then the stable man cautioned that as a respectable citizen, he couldn't be part of a getaway, which he would be if he rented the sleigh now. Fargo settled the matter by drawing his Colt and explaining, "Since you won't have it any other way, just consider this stolen."

That foolishness took a few minutes—enough time for Sheriff Bogardus to ride into town and find out what had just happened to his deputy.

14

Although a whip lay under the ornately curved dash-board of the sleigh, Fargo didn't need it. The high-spirited horses needed no encouragement as they pulled away from Alma. Likely it was because loud noises frightened them. Sheriff Bogardus emptied his pistol at the fleeing fugitives, but from his bowlegged stance in the middle of the street, the lawman's shots flew high.

The shooting quieted, and Father Dyer stuck his head up. "I did hear about the bank robbery in Buck-skin," he said as their sleigh sped up the slick road and the frightened horses' cleated shoes dug out chunks of ice and threw them into Fargo's face. "Mrs. Tabor told me the whole story. I only wish I had been there. Perhaps I could have prevented the false accusation and your unjust imprisonment."

"It would have been nice," Fargo grunted. "Maybe you'll be able to help me out this time around."

"Why are we going to Buckskin? Shouldn't you head for some safer place? I could make my own way there."

"Maybe you could. But I'd like to see you home safe, John. You have your duties to your calling, and that's the way I see my duty to mine. If you can preach at me, then I can make sure you get to your house after I found you all addled in the mountains."

Dyer nodded. The sleigh lurched, and the preacher grabbed the dashboard to keep from falling into Fargo. Dyer looked back as he sat back up.

"Skye, the sheriff is after us."

"Just him, or a posse?"

Dyer stared back for a moment. "Just him. He must

have run to his horse and started after us when he realized that his gunshots missed." For a preacher who was now wanted by the law for helping a dangerous felon escape, Dyer seemed awfully calm and unperturbed.

Hardly daring to take his attention away from the skittish bays, Fargo peeked to the rear. Not more than a hundred yards back, Bogardus spurred a paint pony. The way he was pushing the critter, he'd be within pistol range before long.

The Sharps still had a barrel full of snow, and his Colt had similar problems. Fargo pulled the reins taut to remind the horses that he was still in charge, and reached into his pocket for the deputy's Colt. It still carried three or four rounds.

He turned to Dyer. "Here, you take the reins. I'll see if I can discourage Bogardus."

The preacher saw the pistol in Fargo's gloved hand. "No," he announced firmly. "I'll not be a party to bloodshed."

"One way or another, blood's going to be shed," Fargo shot back. "Why should it be yours?"

Dyer mulled on that and shook his head. Further argument would be useless. The sleigh slowed as they started up a grade. Fargo shook the reins and shouted at them, but they showed little ambition here. Perhaps they didn't understand him. It was likely the first time anybody had hollered at them without using profanity.

Bogardus narrowed the gap, spurring his mount as the surefooted critter galloped toward them.

"John, take the reins. I've got to do something, unless you want to see me at the wrong end of a rope."

"Perhaps justice will prevail," the preacher said.

"And perhaps you'll take up whiskey and I'll take up preaching," Fargo grunted. "Chances are about the same."

Turning, Fargo snapped off a shot at the approaching sheriff. It sailed wide, but came close enough to make Bogardus stay at a more respectful distance for a minute or two.

"No," Dyer insisted. "No more shooting or killing. Enough is enough."

"Well, all right," Fargo shouted. "Now you see it?" He waved the pistol as Dyer's sad eyes followed it. "Now you don't." Fargo turned and heaved the deputy's pistol, hard and straight as he could, at Bogardus.

Dyer grabbed the reins as the thrown pistol caught the sheriff's paint pony square between the ears. "Damn thing never would go straight," Fargo muttered, disappointed because he'd wanted to nail the rider instead of the mount.

The horse stumbled on the slick road. Fargo's hopes rose while its forelegs tangled and Bogardus pitched forward. But the horse recovered its footing quickly. The sheriff managed to sit up straight and fire at the part of Fargo that leaned out of the sleigh.

But the sheriff's bullet whizzed by harmlessly. What pushed Fargo's head back in was a long, limber spruce bough that raked his scalp. Head still down, Fargo looked at the floor and then up at the driver.

"John, rein up some and slow this down a bit."

"But he'll catch up."

"He'll catch up anyway."

Dyer maneuvered the sleigh easily. He'd probably picked up such experience skidding logs in the deep snows of Wisconsin. While he clucked and got the horses to settle into an easier pace, Fargo grabbed the whip off the floor and crouched. He hoped like hell that Dyer would know what to do when the sheriff rode up beside them.

The sleigh bounced and twisted. Fargo glanced up to see why. Dyer sat on the left side of the seat, keeping to that side of the road—so far over that one runner was cutting snow, rather than gliding over the packed surface.

The softer snow beside the road covered rocks, stumps and the like. The resulting bumps jolted the sleigh as well as Fargo's teeth.

But that would force Bogardus to ride up on the opposite side of the sleigh, gun in hand, when he demanded that Dyer stop. Judging by the determined look on the parson's face, that wouldn't even get him to slow down. Dyer nodded to Fargo, and the Trailsman hunkered back down under the dashboard. It pounded and scraped his back while cramps tortured his knees. "In the name of the law, Father Dyer, stop." The shout came from no more than ten or fifteen feet away.

"In the name of a higher law, my son, leave us alone."

Bogardus answered with a high shot, just to let Dyer know he was serious. But so was the preacher, so they kept moving. Not only forward, but more to the left, up the sideslope.

The horse's breath hissed through Fargo's ears. It was almost close enough to feel, for that matter, when Fargo straightened. Grabbing the dashboard with his left hand, he swung the whip furiously with his right.

The whizzing tip caught the astonished Bogardus full on the face. His sudden shock sent a point-blank pistol shot into the snow. A trail of blood ran from his hairline to his receding chin. If the bastard lived through this, he'd be explaining that scar for the rest of his days.

Fargo steadied before the stunned sheriff could bring his gun up, and lashed again. The bullwhip snapped against the sheriff's gun hand with bruising force. His pistol fell to the snow as he shouted something awful about Fargo's mother.

But the whip refused to coil around the sheriff's arm, so that Fargo could jerk the lawman off the horse. "You worthless goddamn motherfucking hellhound," Bogardus shouted, using his stinging hand to pull another pistol from under his coat.

Because the sleigh was so far off to the left, almost entirely in the soft snow, the sheriff had the road to himself. Giving Bogardus an impromptu lesson about sharing, Dyer jerked the reins to the right.

The horses gladly sprang that way, happy to get to where they didn't have to slog through the snow. Bogardus rode along next to the sleigh, which stayed on the sideslope for a moment. The sheriff averted his eyes from Fargo just long enough to see horses directly in front of him. When he looked back, the sleigh was sideslipping toward him.

The paint tried to dodge the menace by moving to

the right. Trouble was, there wasn't much there—about a yard of road, then fifty feet of steep drop-off to the creek. Dyer clucked at the horses and swung the sleigh some more.

Raising a cloud of powder with its scrambling hooves, the sheriff's paint tried to avoid the inevitable. Both horse and rider pitched downward and vanished from the shelf.

It would be at least half an hour before Bogardus caused them any more trouble, if he managed to escape without any broken bones.

"That was some driving, John." The Trailsman sat back down.

"Thank you. I haven't had the opportunity to drive a sleigh for years." Dyer turned and smiled broadly. "I knew there was a way to avoid gunplay."

While they proceeded in a more sensible way toward Buckskin, Fargo studied on their situation. Obviously, Father Dyer was in better shape than he'd figured. The preacher could get home easy enough.

But how in hell was Fargo going to get to Denver? The only way out was back down this little canyon, and if he was lucky, there'd just be a posse and a lynch mob. And what about Dyer's future here?

"John, you'll tell them that I took you hostage and made you drive, won't you?"

The sleigh driver looked over. "No. I won't lie. You saved me, and you've been trying to save yourself. I have nothing to apologize for."

"They're going to be mighty angry."

"So am I. None of this would have happened if they had taken the trouble to learn the truth before they decided to hang you."

"Maybe the church can find a mission for you somewhere else," the Trailsman mused. "I sure wouldn't want to stay around here if I were you."

"I'll go where I'm called," Dyer said. "I'm needed here."

What they needed here and now was a wider road. A single horse was approaching, pulling a shabby carriage that had been converted for winter travel by replacing its wheels with runners.

Dyer courteously found a wide spot and pulled over. After all that excitement on a steady uphill grade, the horses welcomed the opportunity to blow. In the still air, they created a small cloud of fog as the other sleigh approached. It moved slowly downgrade so that the driver had some hope of staying in control and not overrunning the horse.

The Trailsman and the preacher recognized the driver at the same time, but she called out first.

"Father Dyer," the diminutive woman exclaimed. "It's so surprising to see you driving a sleigh, instead of on your snowshoes." Then she recognized the other man. "You! You of all people to be riding with our pastor. Mr. Fargo, I was sure I'd seen the last of you after the sheriff's office burned."

"Mornin', Mrs. Tabor," they both said, doffing their headgear.

"What brings you out of the store today, ma'am?" Dyer added.

"I must go to Tarryall and catch the stage to Denver," she explained. "There are goods to examine and order there, and, well, you know why I must make the trip."

Dyer seemed satisfied with that and exchanged some small talk. His curiosity inspired, Fargo mulled on what he knew of Augusta Tabor. A buying trip made sense—somebody had to select dry goods and notions for the general store, and since womenfolk bought such things, a woman would know what would sell best. But what of the second reason? The one that she and Dyer knew about, and he didn't?

If her trip involved something illegal, or even something that she was keeping hidden from her storekeeper husband, it wasn't likely that she'd be sharing secrets with the preacher. It wasn't beyond imagination that the two might have been friendlier than their reputations allowed, but that wouldn't explain a trip.

While their bays caught their breath and Dyer caught up on the politer gossip of Buckskin, Fargo stared at the tattered carpetbag sitting next to Augusta. It was fair-sized, considering, and not really necessary, given the other luggage back in the boot. And the woman also had a leather purse.

Women tended to hold onto their purses, but hers just lay on the seat. One gloved hand held the reins, and the other clutched the handle on the carpetbag. The way it sagged into the tattered upholstery, it had to be quite heavy.

Augusta had mentioned something about facing down stage robbers, back when she'd explained how she wasn't scared of the jailbreakers she brought dinner to.

Fargo had heard of the trick, now that he studied on it. A goodly number of highwaymen fancied themselves as high-toned rogues, gentlemen of a sort. When they held up a stage, they'd grab the baggage and express, of course, and they'd clean out the male passengers. But they wouldn't bother the women.

Which led some merchants, as well as men with small placer operations, to ship their amalgamated dust and bigger nuggets in a woman's parcel. Not all bandits desired a reputation for manners, of course, so sometimes the gold got taken anyway. But it improved the odds of a safe shipment.

Fargo's suspicion grew to near certainty when he kept staring at the carpetbag. Every time Augusta glanced his way, she got more edgy. So edgy that she cut off the conversation and announced that she really had to be going. "I don't dare miss the stage, pastor. Another storm might blow in any day, and then our home would be cut off from the rest of the world." She shook the reins and clucked to her gray horse.

"Wait, Mrs. Tabor," Fargo hollered.

Exasperation showing on her hewn face, she turned. "What is it, sir?"

"Could you take something to Denver for me?"

"Where in Denver?"

"Clark and Gruber's bank. It shouldn't inconvenience you much, since you're headed there anyway."

"Why would you say that?"

"Mrs. Tabor, you've got a bunch of gold in that carpetbag. I've got a bunch more in my pack. Belongs to a gent over in Oro named Woods, George Woods."

"I know him," she nodded. "So he finally hit something. Glory be!"

"Glad you're so happy about it, ma'am. But could you take his bundle to them and get some money for it?"

"Could I ever. Horace grubstaked Woods so long ago that they've probably both forgotten about it. But I wrote it down. A third of that gold is ours, hallelujah."

Dyer interjected, "I'm sure you'll not forget to tithe, Mrs. Tabor."

Her smile dipped, but then grew even larger. "Of course I shall remember, pastor." Although she marveled at the intricate beauty of the mass of wire gold, she expressed dismay at its weight. But once it was in with the other twenty-five pounds of precious stuff in her carpetbag, the bag was too much for her to lift with one hand, let alone carry. Her purse had room, though. By shifting things some, Augusta ended up with a balanced load that she could tote, purse in one hand and carpetbag in the other.

"One more thing, Mrs. Tabor."

Friendly but impatient, she looked down at Fargo from her perch in her sleigh. "What would that be?"

"Likely you're going to run into a posse that's going to be mighty curious as to our whereabouts."

"Is there something I ought to tell them? Never mind. It wouldn't make any difference. They never listen to me, anyway."

"Just thought you ought to be warned. Have a safe trip."

Dyer uttered his benediction for her journey as she shook the reins and clucked to the horse. Once she was moving, he turned to Fargo. "You really do think they will send a posse after us?"

"After me, anyway." The Trailsman climbed back into their two-horse sleigh, pleased with how effortless it was now that he didn't have that gold on his back. Dyer got aboard and told the horses that it was time to be moving again.

"Hard saying just how long it'll take," Fargo explained. "Bogardus might have to dig himself out of the drifts, get back to the road, and make his way to

Alma before they start coming after us. Or some folks from Alma might take it upon themselves to head this way."

The twisting road climbed into a narrow section of the canyon before Dyer responded. "You don't believe the sheriff might just come after us himself, once he gets up and going?"

"Knowing what lies deep inside people is your business, not mine, John. But I reckon Bogardus has had all of us he can take on his own. He'll fetch some help. Then they'll be after us like dogs on fresh meat."

Dyer nodded. "Sounds reasonable. But will you be safe in Buckskin until they arrive?"

"No." There had to be a deputy or two left in Buckskin who'd recognize Skye Fargo as the bank robber who'd escaped two weeks ago. Plus, there were all manner of normal townfolk who'd have the same memory. And Daisy Melrose had already threatened to kill him; there wasn't any reason why she wouldn't want to try again.

But unless a man sprouted wings or took up winter mountain climbing, there was only one way into or out of Buckskin Joe: the narrow road they were on now. As a place to be running to, it didn't make a lot of sense. But it was home to Father Dyer, and Fargo had taken it upon himself to make sure the preacher got there. If Fargo jumped out here and made his own way, surely Dyer could get on into Buckskin. The man had been doing fine all morning.

The Trailsman looked over at the frontier parson. Dyer's face was animated as he deftly persuaded the horses to continue onward and upward. But Fargo could see paleness and fatigue, too. The gent had been knocked out by the force of a snowslide, and then he'd stayed up all night. Resolutely, Fargo decided to go on to Buckskin Joe and make sure the preacher arrived home. Something just didn't sit right about abandoning Dyer, even this close.

Fargo squinted upward. For almost two thousand vertical feet on their left, a steep slope climbed from the snow-packed roadway. The lower half sat below timberline. Most of its trees had been logged, although a few determined spruce and aspen poked through the snow. Above that, there was nothing but snow up to the crest, a rocky windswept ridge.

What made the spectacle more than scenery was the way the snow sat up near the top. It looked just like the stuff near the summit of Mosquito Pass—a wall of wind-packed cornices that could give way any moment, starting an avalanche. Even if it didn't hit anybody, a snowslide here meant considerable problems getting into and out of Buckskin Joe.

Fargo hoped Dyer was praying hard as they came through this stretch. The brutal cold weather that always followed storms seemed to be lifting. Welcome as sunshine and warmth were, the improved weather meant that the looming snowpacks would grow more unstable by the moment.

The Trailsman reached back in his gear and pulled out the Sharps carbine as Dyer drove on. With its cleaning rod, he pushed most of the snow out of the barrel, and a swab took care of the remaining moisture.

"Are you just tending to your gear, Skye?" Dyer asked after they got past the narrowest spot. "Or . . . ?"

"I'm not planning to shoot at anybody, John," Fargo answered. This looked like as good a spot as any. "Stop for a minute. I need to see if this still shoots straight after all the abuse it's got."

Dyer reined up and Fargo got out, aiming the gun high.

"An odd target, Skye," Dyer commented as he stepped out. "So distant that you'll have trouble telling whether you hit anything."

Taking careful aim at the vertical edge of a cornice, Fargo pulled the trigger. A sharp crack thundered from the carbine.

As best as Fargo could tell, his rifle remained reliable. But the sound of the gun got there before the bullet did. The target shifted and shook, emitting small puffclouds of snow that made it difficult to see where the heavy bullet might have hit.

Dyer looked puzzled when Fargo loaded another round. "What are you trying to do, start an avalanche?"

Fargo pulled the trigger. This time, the cornice crumbled into the snowfield at its foot. With an ominous rumble, the mass of snow began its slide toward the canyon floor.

Both men watched agape as the sliding snow funneled into a narrow natural chute somewhere near timberline, then roared on downward. They couldn't see its arrival at the canyon floor, since that was around a bend, but the roar stopped, and then a powdery cloud rose.

Fargo turned to the preacher. "You're right, John. I was trying to start an avalanche. Best way I know of to slow that posse down."

"But someone might have been caught in it . . ."

"Not likely. There wasn't anybody within two miles of us from the rear. Mrs. Tabor's long past. Who's left?"

"Still . . ." The preacher turned to Fargo, glowing of righteousness. "You shouldn't take such risks. I don't feel right being a party to this." Dyer grabbed the sleigh railing to steady himself.

Fargo climbed back onto the plush seat, and lent Dyer a hand. The minister was as tough as a frontier preacher had to be. But he'd been through plenty in the last twenty-four hours, including a concussion. Concussions were peculiar and unpredictable. In moments, an alert and energetic man could be incoherent and trembling. Dyer wasn't at that point, but he showed considerably less ambition than he had when they'd pulled over.

Fargo shook the reins and the horses started the last two miles to town. They'd be the last horses that came through for several days—until the slide got dug out, or somebody managed to carve a route over it. Dyer sat silently, resting up.

Smoke poured from the chimney of Daisy's two-story cathouse on the edge of town, and the ground still shook from the stamp mill. Except for the dirty snow that had been trampled and pushed around, Buckskin Joe hadn't changed worth mention since the first time Fargo had ridden in. Well, there was a gap between buildings where there had been a sheriff's office. But Fargo sure didn't have any trouble tending to his first order of business—getting some hot food inside himself and his companion.

Although every patron in the tiny greasy-spoon diner seemed to know Father Dyer well enough to greet him upon their entry, nobody appeared to notice or mention that their pastor's companion looked a lot like the gent who'd busted out of their jail just before the sheriff's office burned.

The venison stew and coffee worked like medicine on the tired preacher, who was stepping quite nimbly by the time they got out the door. Their borrowed sleigh sat just up the street, so Dyer ought to be back in his cabin before long.

One barrel-shaped gent, who sported a black steer-horn mustache glistening with the wax that kept its tips sharp, had other ideas, though. The jasper also sported a star, pinned on the outside of his corduroy coat.

Fargo noticed all that when he heard "Hey, you" from behind, and spun in his tracks, ready to draw or dive as the situation demanded. In the process, he almost knocked the deputy over. The fellow had padded up close before hollering, and he already had his gun out.

"What's your problem?" Fargo asked wearily. Dyer sidestepped a bit before turning.

"My goddamn problem? You're the one with a goddamn problem, pardner."

The steam rose a couple notches in Father Dyer, but he didn't say anything. The righteous way he stared at the impious deputy was expression enough. Any second now he might cut loose with all Ten Commandments.

"Now, why would I have a problem?" Fargo rejoined. "I'm just accompanying Father Dyer on his rounds."

"Oh, oh, what?" The deputy's brown eyes moved over to the parson. "Excuse my language, Father Dyer." Then back to Fargo. "You're a wanted man. There's even a bounty on you." He emitted a sardonic chuckle. "I don't care if you're standing next to Jesus Christ himself, you're either going to come to jail so as we

160

can hang you, or you're going to die right here if you don't act peaceable."

"Not much of a choice, is it?" Fargo mused aloud. "Say, how much is the bounty?"

"A thousand dollars, dead or alive. The town fathers put it up after you broke jail and set the sheriff's office on fire. They were just getting ready to put up the posters and send out the fliers."

Dyer interrupted. "A thousand dollars? Wait, young man. I believe that I captured him."

The deputy swallowed hard and turned to the preacher. "What? Listen, padre, you stay out of what isn't your business."

"Oh, you'd get your fair share," Dyer explained, his voice beginning to boom as it gained timbre. "At least thirty pieces of silver."

Fargo's uppercut rocked the deputy's shiny mustache back, along with the rest of his head. The man reeled, bringing up his pistol. The Trailsman chopped his chubby arm, forcing the revolver to fall. An instant later, Dyer's roundhouse right, delivered by a ham-sized fist, put the deputy down with his gun.

"Oh my," Dyer wondered aloud. "What if someone saw that? What would they think of me?"

There had been folks moving along the street, so Fargo had the same concern, although for different reasons. Grabbing Dyer's arm, he tugged the preacher into the narrow slot between the diner and the next building, an assay office. The passage was so narrow that they had to sidestep all the way back to the alley.

Even there, they had company. The broad-shouldered but stooped gent coming their way looked just as annoyed as they did at having someone else around. His big soup-strainer mustache didn't keep him from appearing sheepish.

"Why, Mayor Tabor," Fargo proclaimed. "Fancy meeting you here in an alley in broad daylight."

The storekeeper gulped in some fresh air as his face reddened. It almost glowed when he saw that Fargo's companion was the Rev. John L. Dyer.

"Ahem," Tabor finally said after considerable hemming and hawing. "Good afternoon, pastor. And good day to you, sir. I don't believe I know you."

"We met in your store just before the bank robbery, Hod. Never did get a chance to shake before all the ruckus started."

"Oh yes," the slack-jawed storekeeper recalled. "Then you're the one—the one we just posted a reward for." Tabor turned and tried to sound indignant. "Father Dyer what on earth you doing with this criminal?"

"Our Lord Jesus associated with publicans and sinners, Horace."

Fargo broke in. "And just what might you be doing, skulking down an alley in daylight?"

Tabor muttered it really wasn't anybody's business, although he had a perfectly good reason. Something to do with town government, like checking to see if folks were picking up their trash. Nobody ever did, of course, because this was a mining camp. But for six months of the year, at least, nobody ever noticed, since a fresh layer of snow covered the yards full of moldy busted tack, rusting barrel hoops, rotting mule corpses, and anything else that couldn't be used as firewood.

"Confession is good for the soul, Hod," Fargo advised. "Isn't that so, Father Dyer?"

The parson nodded while Tabor stood there, perplexed and terrified that the vicious outlaw in front of him would pull out a gun.

"Well, Hod, I'll confess that I busted out of your jail. And that I ended up setting your sheriff's office on fire. But I reckon I can explain most of it."

"You'd get your chance in court. Really, you would," Tabor insisted.

"That's as may be, Hod. But I've done my confessing for today. Anything on your mind?"

Tabor shook his head and just looked confused.

"Gee, Hod, I thought you'd tell us. So I guess I'll have to talk for you. You know, Mrs. Tabor's a fine woman. The pastor here may dispute this, but she comes closer to acting Christian than anybody else I've run across in this two-bit ramshackle town of yours."

Tabor shifted uneasily. "Why, yes, of course. She's an angel."

"Too good for the likes of you, Hod. You saw her off on the sleigh this morning, on her way to Tarryall to catch the Denver stage. And I bet it wasn't twenty minutes later that you were over at Daisy Melrose's."

"Horace!" Dyer fixed a doomful look on the errant member of his flock, who found something mighty interesting in the way his boots shuffled in the soggy snow.

"She runs a business here," Tabor tried to explain. "I was just, ah, er, checking on . . ."

"Checking on how well she bounced on that four-poster." Fargo finished the sentence for him.

Shamefaced, Tabor looked at Dyer. "It'll be my ruin if Augusta ever learns of this. And my political career. I was going to stand for the territorial legislature, and no, no, I couldn't. What am I going to do? It was all I could do to keep Daisy from . . ."

"You mean she was blackmailing you, too." Fargo sighed. "Well, Hod, you know what a vicious criminal I am. And I'm right sure your pastor won't have much trouble coming up with a topic for next Sunday's sermon."

Dyer turned from Tabor. "No, I suppose I won't." Rather than stentorian, his voice now sounded muted and sad.

"Tell you what, Hod," Fargo offered. "I'll forget that I saw you here if you'll forget that you saw me here. Deal?"

Tabor stuck out his hand and they shook on it. Then he turned to Dyer. "She'll leave me if she ever finds out."

The pastor shrugged his massive shoulders. "If she learns, it won't be from me." In step with the Trails-man, he started walking on down the alley as Tabor shuffled off the other way.

"I guess you won't be troubled by the local authorities now," Dyer surmised.

"I wouldn't bet on it, John. He'll stew on that for about an hour, and then he's going to round up all the law and guns he can find, and come after me. You've got a professional obligation not to mention what you've just heard, and nobody that matters around this town has yet believed a word I say."

When they reached the cross street, Dyer edged over to the main thoroughfare and came back, driving the sleigh. The knocked-out deputy had been hauled inside the restaurant. Whenever he came to, and whenever various realizations dawned on Tabor, Buckskin Joe figured to get a lot more lively.

Without too much difficulty, Dyer got the team going up the steep road—more like a trail—that led half a mile to his modest cabin. Fargo fetched the preacher's gear while the pastor went inside and started a fire. On the last trip, Dyer met him at the doorway.

"The only pay I can offer is my gratitude for your help and my prayers for your continued well-being, Skye."

Fargo nodded and stuck out his hand. "We don't see eye to eye on a lot of things, John. But you're some man to travel with. You don't back down and you keep your word." Fargo looked down at the man's huge right hand. "And you're pretty good with your fists, too. I'm gonna have to see you in a pulpit some day."

"That would be pay enough." Dyer grinned. Then his face fell a bit. "Where are you off to, Skye? Or is it something I shouldn't know?"

"I'll get this sleigh back to town, and then, well, I'll figure out some way out of here before they hang me."

"Oh, the sleigh," Dyer said. "Check the off horse. He was stepping peculiarly. Probably something in his shoe. Here, I'll help."

The bay must have been ticklish. When Dyer knelt next to its right rear hoof, it came up and caught him on the shoulder, rolling the big preacher back in the snow. Fargo jumped to Dyer's side.

He was out again. Or maybe worse, the shallow, ragged way he was breathing.

"Shit. Damn. Hell. Goddamn." Fargo continued for a minute or so, letting loose his first full-powered cussing since he'd found the preacher by the snow-slide. It didn't feel quite as good as it should have.

Then the Trailsman studied on what came next.

Most anybody in town would be glad to tend the preacher, no doubt. But he didn't have friends worth mention down there, even at the whorehouse, so it'd be a matter of knocking on strangers' doors in a town where they were tacking up Wanted posters with his name on them.

His wary eyes scanned the hillside and caught a plume of smoke coming out of such trees as remained a quarter mile away. Brightening, he wrestled Dyer into the sleigh and told the team to behave themselves.

The petite blond dancer with the beautiful face answered her door in a robe while holding a derringer.

"Oh, Skye, it's you. You're back." Her embrace nearly toppled him.

"Easy," Fargo cautioned. "I've got a sick man with me. I'll bring him in."

Dyer was a big man, no easier to move now than he had been a couple minutes ago. Hoping that he wouldn't slip in the snow, Fargo got Dyer's massive arms over his shoulders and hoisted the preacher onto his back. A vagrant rock lurking under the snow caught his ankle and threatened to send them both into a drift, but Fargo recovered in time and got Dyer onto the overstuffed ottoman.

"My God, you've brought Father Dyer into my house," she exclaimed once she'd gotten a look at the gent on her sofa. "What happened to him?"

"A lot of things," Fargo replied. "He got stunned yesterday. Generally, he's fairly chipper, but any time something hits him, he goes out like a lamp. Reckon he just needs somebody to watch him while he rests up."

Silver Heels shook her golden curls. "I've done some nursing. But why can't you stay?"

Fargo explained his problem. The only good part about the current situation was that Tabor would send men up to Dyer's cabin first, since he was Fargo's last known companion. Since smoke was still coming out its chimney from the warming fire the preacher had started, they might wait around there for some time, unwilling to shoot. But even in that crowd, somebody would eventually get smart enough to suggest following the sleigh tracks.

"So you can't stay and keep company with me? This is my night off."

Fargo shook his head. "I've got to get out of here or you're going to be in danger."

"Pooh," she said. "Those miners all adore me. And they all respect the preacher."

Hearing a rustle to his side, Fargo turned from the heaving Dyer. Silver Heels was unbuttoning her robe; the swell of her luscious breasts was already apparent, and growing more luscious with every undone button.

"Okay, you talked me into staying for a few minutes," Fargo conceded, sweeping her up into his arms and transporting her to the bedroom.

Her china-blue eyes sparkled as Fargo slid one hand under the robe, cupping a breast, while the other worked on the buttons. Her own were busy on his coat, then his shirt, and finally his trousers.

"Oh, Skye," she sighed as she rolled back, naked and as ready as a woman ever got, "I want all of you."

In a moment, Fargo was as warm and comfortable as he'd been for some time. She cocked her legs up in the air. Her smooth thighs were lean, but strong from dancing. She used that strength to lever him down into her, deep and straight.

Fargo plunged into the opportunity, pushing her down while she matched with upward bounds. Their feverish rhythm quickened to a staccato pace, then got even faster and hotter.

Dancing gals must be stronger than he'd thought, Fargo mused as they pounded on. But then again, he'd been up all night listening to a sermon, at that. He had a right to feel a little peakèd.

Amazing, though, how energized a man could feel under these circumstances. The brutal world out there of blood-lust lynch mobs and shit-heel deputies and politically ambitious storekeepers vanished into his pulsing desire to push himself inside Silver Heels. Not just push, immerse. Deeper. Harder. Faster.

Driven by her gasps and unquenched passion, Fargo made his final push, then felt her shudder as his eruption drove her to an ecstasy bigger than the mountains outside. The supple dancer twisted and bucked, her waving feet now trying to scrape the ceiling.

"Oh, Fargo, I knew it would be this wonderful when you came again," she exulted when they calmed down, still entwined. They stayed that way, grasping each other.

Then she pushed a deep kiss at him that he couldn't back away from even if he'd wanted to. Meanwhile, he learned that she had strong, lithe muscles all over; the gentle but firm massage from deep inside was stirring his organ into new vigor.

Slow and easy, they started anew. Taking their time, they rolled around on the bed. For a spell, she sat atop, her voluptuous breasts bouncing in the soft afternoon light as Fargo just relaxed back and enjoyed the show. When she bent down, Fargo wrestled his willing partner to her side. They fluttered together like a gull's wings as their intensity grew and burst into a heaving, thrashing culmination.

Drained, Fargo started to roll over, mulling the possibilities for spending the night there. A wind-up alarm clock caught his eye; it was only two in the afternoon.

Glumly, he sat up. There were things that he had to do yet in Buckskin Joe. And if he stayed at Silver Heels's cabin, or anywhere nearby, the odds were against his living long enough to do what he had to.

"Don't tell me that you are going to just up and disappear, the way you did last time."

"Then I won't tell you that, honey. But that's what'll likely happen. You recall the great bank robbery that failed?"

She nodded, and grew tearful when she learned that the Skye Fargo who'd been in her bed that rainy morning was the same man now wanted hereabouts. "You just take good care of Father Dyer, honey, okay? Make sure he rests up and gets some food."

"He'll not be comfortable here for very long," Silver Heels objected. "Why, it would ruin his reputation if word got out that he spent a night here, even if . . ."

"His reputation's strong enough to take it," Fargo replied as he finished dressing. "By tomorrow, doubtless, he can walk down to his cabin. And then you can get word to the respectable folk that they ought to check up on him until he's got all his steam back."

The dancer nodded. "I'll do that. Where are you going?"

"Don't hold supper for me," Fargo answered as he finished swabbing out his Colt. He stepped out her door and wished that Dyer was up and about. The preacher knew considerable more about maneuvering sleighs, especially getting one to turn around in such a tight space. But the Trailsman managed, although the damn thing was pretty heavy to be shoving around.

His first stop was Dyer's cabin, where wisps of smoke still rose from the stovepipe. More precisely, the horses stopped the sleigh there when somebody hollered from the trees. Fargo had rolled out about a hundred yards before that.

Two deputies had come up from town, and they had the cabin flanked as they lurked in the snowdrifts amid the brush. But both men were looking puzzled at the empty sleigh. The uphill one knew about Fargo's presence for the split second between the moment a pistol butt hit his ear and the moment he sagged into the snow.

Fargo had been quiet about it, but not quiet enough. The loud-mouthed downhill one hollered. "Hey, Mike, what's going on? I heard somethin' up by you?"

"Come over and find out," Fargo replied, Colt drawn.

The bushes shook and a wary deputy looked up past the cabin. They recognized each other, since they'd met earlier that day and the nasty bump on the deputy's head was still growing. If it got any bigger or darker, nobody'd notice his shiny black waxed mustache.

"You!" the dumb shit shouted, slapping leather.

"Me," Fargo answered as he poked a slug into the man's chest. The surprised deputy rocked back and collapsed atop the snow, which began to turn pink as his life seeped into it.

Fargo shook his head and holstered his Colt. You couldn't say that Sheriff Bogardus didn't hire deputies with courage. But they could have used more common sense and common courtesy.

The Trailsman parked the sleigh up the street from Tabor's store, and went around to the alley, then past the woodshed and up to the back door.

"The two deputies are up at Father Dyer's cabin," Tabor was explaining to the half-dozen men sitting by the stove. "They'll keep him there until the sheriff gets back from Alma. Then Bogardus can figure out what to do."

"Might be a while," somebody commented. "Damn road's blocked by a slide."

That seemed as good a time as any to walk on in.

"Good afternoon, your honor," Fargo told the mayor. "Am I interrupting something?"

The astonished Tabor's jaw dropped. "How'd you get here?"

"Rode some, walked some. Usual way folks get around. There a problem with that?" Fargo scanned the room. It was occupied by the town fathers. That kind of men had their faults, certainly, but they weren't prone to rash acts, either. They cared about their businesses and their families, which meant they cared about staying alive.

"Wh-what are you going to do?" the hardware dealer asked.

"Well, you gents all think that I tried to rob the bank across the street, right?"

They stayed frozen like so many statues. But when Tabor finally nodded without getting his head shot off, the rest joined in the motion.

Fargo looked up at the wall clock. It was only two-thirty, half an hour before the bank would close, so he had a little time to spare. He mentioned to the man next to the stove that he'd like some coffee.

Tin cup in one hand and Colt in the other, Fargo explained some facts to his attentive audience. "Three of those robbers died across the street that afternoon. I was the one that killed them, shooting through the front window here. That bloodstain over there's mine."

They followed his pointing Colt. "I got cut up by the glass and otherwise banged up," Fargo continued. "When I came around, I was in your jail, and you planned to hang me. Now, I was just a stranger passing through, same as now. All I did was keep your bank from getting robbed."

To his neighbor, Tabor whispered, "That's what Augusta said."

"She saw it right," Fargo said. "But now that I'm wanted over half the territory for bank robbery, I'd best earn the reputation. Right? You gents have a ringside seat on this one."

"You'll never get away with it," the hardware dealer cautioned.

"Sure, you guys will be sitting right here. And some of you no doubt have guns. But I don't reckon you'll use 'em, because my old buddy Hod here is coming along." Fargo grabbed the mayor and twisted his arm back. Tabor didn't try to twist away. He had too much respect for the pistol pointed at his ear.

Robbing Griswold's Bank of Buckskin Joe was so easy that Fargo began to wonder why he hadn't taken up a life of crime. He walked in with Tabor right at closing time. While the cashier cowered in a corner, the two tellers gladly cooperated to fill a canvas sack with all the money it would hold—at least forty pounds of the stuff.

Back on the street, with Tabor frog-stepping before him, Fargo waved at the men watching from the store.

"Reckon these horses can get over that slide down the road, Hod?" Fargo prodded the mayor into the sleigh.

"I-I don't know. Maybe."

"Guess we'll find out. You drive." Fargo settled in, his Colt at Tabor's side. Tabor clucked and the horses started down the street, toward Daisy's house and then the canyon.

"No need to hurry, Mayor. Who's gonna come after us?" Fargo asked the terrified Tabor.

Tabor shook his head. "Nobody, I guess. I just reckoned you would be in a hurry."

"Nah. Time to relax, now. You got a cigar?"

The mayor reached into his vest and pulled out a stogy. Fargo bit its end off. Bending down, he got it lit, and almost choked on its vile taste. But he wouldn't need it long.

They were clear of town, now. He poked Tabor with the pistol. "I'm done with you now. Jump off, or I'll shoot you off." Tabor seemed pleased enough to get off on his own.

As soon as the spluttering mayor was out of sight, Fargo stopped the sleigh on a slick, hard-packed spot where no tracks would show. He got out and approached the off horse cautiously, patting it and consoling it. Then he jammed the lit cigar under its tail strap and jumped back.

With a fire under its tail, the pesky critter tried to take off for the moon. That being impossible, it settled on Alma. No doubt its partner was confused, but when one horse in a team starts moving, the other one doesn't have much choice but to move, too. At the rate they were going, they'd sail right over that snow-slide, and the posse on the other side could try to figure it all out.

15

The next morning, Fargo woke from a deep sleep in an empty bed. He wasn't too concerned, since the spot where Silver Heels had been sleeping next to him was still warm. In fact, he could hear her out in the front room.

"Oh, Father Dyer, you're looking much better."

The preacher moaned some, the way men do when they're waking up, and then recognized his nurse.

"The dancing girl? Where am I?"

"In my parlor," she answered.

Dyer let her know that he wasn't at all pleased by that. He still looked grumpy when Fargo walked into the room. "Easy, now, John. She's a lot better nurse-maid than I am, and you looked pretty ragged after that horse kicked you."

Dyer settled back into the couch. "I suppose so. But, what will people think?"

"Doubt anybody knows."

The preacher stood up and stretched, then realized he was clad only in a patched wool union suit. Blushing, he retreated to the couch and pulled a blanket over himself while Silver Heels tried to keep from laughing. She finally had to leave the room.

"How you feeling, John?"

"Skye, I don't know whether to laugh or cry. Here I am, a minister of the gospel, and I've just spent the night in the home of a notorious trollop. And I've been traveling with a man wanted for, well, for everything except leprosy, I think."

"Glad you're up and about, John. I'll be glad to walk you down to your place. I'd like to borrow those skis of yours."

"You're welcome to them," Dyer said. "I have several pair. They're easy to make if you know how to steam the ends to get them bent." He started pulling on his clothes, looking furtively toward the bedroom in case he might be seen by Silver Heels. As he got inside his trousers, he looked up at Fargo. "Why would you want to borrow my skis?"

"To make my getaway from a bank robbery," Fargo answered calmly.

Dyer seemed to think it was a joke. From his cabin door, he even wished Fargo Godspeed as the Trailsman, poling with two fresh aspen stubs, kicked and glided away, following the contour of the hillside with thousands of stolen dollars on his back. "I'm headed for Oro, John," Fargo called back. "If I can make it, so can you with your mail route."

"God be with you," Dyer shouted before retreating to his small but warm cabin.

The preacher must have had friends in high places, for the high places turned out to be more friendly than Fargo had anticipated. Following pretty much the same route as he and Sedgwick and Polly had taken one night, Fargo gained confidence on the skis, only falling a couple times.

Climbing to the ridge before the pass with a load on his back and ten pounds on each foot was tedious. At first it was exhausting as Fargo tried the herringbone pattern, then sidestepping. Sweating profusely despite the chill in the thin air, he recalled his traverse efforts on the hill above Alma. Making his own zigzag switchback trail, and keeping his pace sensible, he gained the crest.

The sight of the vast barren sweep left by the avalanche at the top of Mosquito Pass made him mindful as he shuffled along the sidehill to the notch. Like everything else in nature, snow held a pattern, a pattern that a man could learn how to read. And then he'd know when it was stable and when it wasn't. But how to learn it? And who the hell wanted to stay in the snow long enough to learn to read it?

Exhilarated, Fargo made the eight downhill miles from the summit to Oro City in less than an hour, while the sun sank behind the Sawatch Range to the west. He hadn't really expected to get there earlier—in fact, he was pleasantly surprised at how quickly he got around on skis in these mountains—but it would have simplified matters.

As it was, he had to nose around Oro for a good twenty minutes before learning that Griswold wasn't in his bank, since the building stood dark and empty. Nor was he at home, unless his dumpy wife was given to telling shameful lies. And the gent couldn't be found in the hotel, either.

So Fargo shattered the window of one of the town's only other business establishments with a pistol shot.

As soon as the scream from the woman inside subsided, Fargo shouted, "Hey, Griswold!"

A man hollered something about there being a dangerous lunatic with a gun out there in the snow. The voice was Griswold's, though.

"Meet you at your bank in fifteen minutes. See you there."

When the panting and pissed-off banker arrived, Fargo told his half-wit bodyguard to go for a walk. "Or even better," the Trailsman concluded, tossing him a double eagle of Griswold's money, "go down to the hotel and get shit-faced drunk." The man looked helplessly at his boss, who shrugged, then lit off down the street.

"What is this?" Griswold demanded. "There's barely two nickels in there if you've got robbery on your mind, Fargo. They've been running on the bank all day."

Fargo shook his head, although it was too dark for Griswold to see the motion. "No, Griswold. But I'd take it kind if you opened up. Got a proposition for you I need to discuss in private, if you catch my drift."

Griswold fished some keys out of his pocket and started working on the three deadbolt locks. "I know. You want to blackmail me."

Fargo pushed the Colt against his heaving side. "Reckon I could. But I hate to cut in on somebody else's trade, and Miss Daisy Melrose over in Buckskin has been doing a fine job of that, all on her own, hasn't she?"

With an eerie creak, the heavy door swung open. "How'd you know? Did that bitch tell you?"

Fargo stepped in behind the banker. Instead of answering, he moved on with the conversation. "She's a hardhearted gal that likes to run things. Everything, as a matter of fact. No doubt she's been putting some heat on you to foreclose a little sooner than you might otherwise have, and then she buys up the notes and sets up for a comfortable retirement."

The banker padded through the lobby to his office. With Fargo at his side, he lit a coal-oil lamp. Just the smell of it brought back sickening memories, but the Trailsman pushed that out of his mind. Griswold's motions seemed to be asking if they could sit down, so Fargo nodded.

"You sure figured out a lot of things fast, mister," the trembling banker said as he settled into his plush chair. "What are you up to?"

"On that account, precious little," Fargo chuckled. "You and Hod Tabor and I don't know who all else are the ones that have to stay around and figure that one out. I've got other fish to fry."

"What?"

Fargo emptied the canvas bag on Griswold's desk. A boisterous cascade of gold coins rolled out in a heap, some chiming as they fell to the floor. Several wads of greenbacks fluttered out as Fargo finished shaking the bag.

"That's the money from your Buckskin bank," Fargo explained. "It ought to keep you solvent here for a spell."

"But-but how?" the perplexed banker wondered.

"Let's just say it was an unauthorized withdrawal," Fargo explained. "Though folks over there might say it was a bank robbery. But they don't see very well over in Buckskin. They thought I tried to rob it last time around, when I was the one that stopped three of the robbers."

Griswold's head fell. "That was awful." He looked around, then up. "I owe you for this job."

"That you do," Fargo said, accepting a handful of

bills. The Trailsman stood there, unmoving, and Griswold got confused again. "Isn't that it?"

"No, you still owe me. You're going to clear all the paper that's out on me, for one thing."

Griswold nodded. "I can do that. Anything else?"

"Isn't it traditional to offer a reward to someone who prevents a bank robbery?"

Griswold swallowed hard and slumped. "I suppose so. What would be fair?"

"Fetch me the notes or liens or whatevers on the Ragged Ass Mine and the C Bar S Ranch."

"But Woods still owes. And, honest, I had nothing to do with that missing ore, even if that suspicious prospector says otherwise."

"Not disputing your word, Griswold. But they're honest folk. Paper or not, they'll pay you up as soon as they can. Woods will be coming into a considerable sum shortly, anyway. You can rest easy on that account."

"This is most irregular," Griswold complained as he reached into a deep drawer of the rolltop desk.

"Don't even think about turning around with that baby pistol," Fargo cautioned. "Just give me the papers."

The glum banker reached into another drawer and brought out two folders, which he handed to Fargo.

"You'd best lock up behind me while you put that money away," the Trailsman announced on his way out. "That pile of cash might tempt some poor man with a weaker nature than mine."

Even in the night, under the light of just a sliver of a moon, getting around on skis was easier than he had ever thought it would be, since he'd first seen these leaning against a tree over on the other side of the Mosquito Range. The miles seemed to glide by as Fargo slid along the snow-covered valley, staying close by the gurgling infant that was growing into the Arkansas River.

Comfortable as these skis were getting, though, it was still damn good to see the Ovaro in the corral. The big pinto nickered in recognition as Fargo patted his muzzle and assured him that they were headed for warm and sunny Texas.

But the other horses started a fuss. Fargo's keen ears picked up noises in the ranch house, followed by the creak of a door that no doubt had a gun pointed out it. Jim Sedgwick was just a kid, but he was a cowboy who took horse theft seriously.

"What's going on out there?" he shouted, trying to sound good and gruff.

"Easy, Jim. This is Fargo. I'm just fetching my pinto. I'll be riding on here shortly."

"Shee-it, Fargo. Why didn't you come to the door so as we could coffee you up? Ain't proper at all to just flit by like this."

Well, why not? Lamps got lit and the house stirred with two busy women scurrying to find some dinner for the late-arriving guest. Fargo hadn't realized how tired he really was—that skiing felt good while it was going, but it sure pulled the starch out of man—until he got comfortable at the kitchen table. He started yawning while explaining how they wouldn't have to worry about Griswold anymore.

Although he tried to give the honor to one of them, they insisted that he shove the two folders into the stove. Shortly thereafter, Jim got the yawns bad himself and mentioned something about feeding cows at sunrise. He shuffled off to bed.

Anna and Prudence just sat there at the table. Finally Prudence spoke. "You going to decide, Fargo? Or do we have to flip a coin to see who gets you first?"

LOOKING FORWARD!

**The following is the opening
section from the next novel in the exciting
Trailsman series from Signet:**

THE TRAILSMAN # 76
WILDCAT WAGONS

*1860, south of Pikes Peak, where the
Sangre de Cristo mountains spill
from Colorado into the turbulent territory
called New Mexico . . .*

"Put that thing down, honey. It might go off," the
big man with the lake-blue eyes said, his voice calm.

"It will go off, and put a hole right through you,
unless you do what I say," the girl snapped, and the big
man's eyes narrowed as he peered hard at her. He saw
light-brown hair and eyes to match, a small, straight nose
in a pretty face with soft cheeks and nicely curved lips.
But the eyes were as determined as the thrust of her jaw.

"Get off the horse," she said, and he eyed the
heavy, breech-loading Henry leveled at him. She held
the rifle without a quiver, and the big man slowly
swung one leg from the saddle and landed lightly on
the balls of his feet. The rifle followed him, he saw,
and he cursed silently. The trip had been pleasantly

peaceful and easy riding until the girl had exploded out of the trees, the rifle already held on him.

"You're too damn pretty to be playing highwayman, honey," he offered.

"I'm not playing highwayman," she snapped back, and he let his eyes roam across a tan shirt covering smallish breasts, a small waist and trim legs in tight Levi's and he returned his gaze to the determined, tight face.

"Then you're making some kind of mistake," he said.

"No mistake. You're the Trailsman—Skye Fargo," she countered.

"One for you," Fargo said with some surprise.

"And you're on your way to General Taylor to break trail for his wagon train."

"Two for you," Fargo grunted, and felt surprise again.

"I'm going on that train. I'm going to be part of it and you're going to see to it."

"The hell I am."

"You'll see to it or else," she said tightly, and Fargo saw the big old Henry still didn't waver. But he felt the irritation spiraling inside him.

"I've heard enough, girlie. You move on before I get real mad," he said and started to turn back to the Ovaro. The shot exploded and he felt the rush of air as the bullet almost grazed his cheek. Instinctively, he twisted, went down on one knee and reached for the sixgun at his side.

"Don't, dammit," her voice snapped out. He halted, his hand frozen in midair and he eyed the big Henry aimed directly at his chest. Slowly he drew his hand back from the butt of the Colt and pushed to his feet, his eyes now cold as a lake in midwinter.

"What are you all about?" Fargo frowned.

"What I'm about is being part of that wagon train and I'll pay you three hundred dollars to make that happen," she said.

Fargo's lips pursed at the offer. "That's a lot of

money," he remarked. "But I can't make you part of anything."

"Yes, you can. He needs you. He'll go along with whatever you ask. You promise to include me, that's all."

"Sorry, I can't do that."

"Dammit, you can. You include me or you'll never break another trail for anybody," she said, her voice rising.

"How'll that help you?" Fargo questioned calmly.

"He'll have to get somebody else and I'll get them to include me," she tossed back, and Fargo's eyes peered into her. She was not as hard as she tried to make herself out to be. That showed in the whiteness of her knuckles that gripped the rifle and in the tiny lines of nervousness that touched the corners of her mouth. There was desperation behind her hardness and he put reasonableness into his voice.

"You're being real dumb. I could agree now and not mean one damn word of it. Talk's cheap," Fargo said.

"You wouldn't do that. You're not the kind. You'd stay by your word."

"How do you know that about me?"

"I know, just leave it at that."

"How'd you know it was me riding the road?"

"I knew you rode a real handsome Ovaro and you were due," she answered. Fargo took in the rifle again. It hadn't wavered an inch and her knuckles were still white. "Well, will you give me your word?" she pressed.

He let thoughts whirl inside him for a long moment. "Looks as though you and that big old Henry don't give me much choice but to do what you want," he said with a resigned shrug. He saw her breasts push tiny points into the shirt with the deep rush of breath she let hiss from her.

"Then I'll look for you in Claysville," she said, and backed the brown mare away from him without lowering the rifle.

"Wait," Fargo said. "Aren't you going to tell me anything about yourself?"

"When the time comes," the girl said, and continued to back away. Suddenly, she yanked the mare to the left and sent the horse racing into the trees. Fargo waited for a few moments and listened to her riding up through the hillside. When the sound of her had died away, he swung onto the Ovaro and turned the horse up through the trees. He felt the anger simmering inside him as he quickly picked up her trail, hoofprints fresh and clear in the soft ground, leaves pressed down, grass and moss clearly marked with the edges of the hooves. She'd not only threatened him, almost shot his ear off, and tried to force him into wild promises, but she seemed to know more about him than she ought. Now it'd be his turn to demand answers, he vowed as he followed her prints where she'd made a wide circle up a gentle slope, stayed in the trees, and finally started down the other side to a road below.

Fargo stayed higher on the slope and caught sight of her, moving the Ovaro forward to stay above her and slightly behind as she continued down the slope. She rode slowly, absorbed in her own thoughts. Fargo took the lariat from the fork swell and lifted the rope above his head. He sent the rope into an easy, graceful spin, pushed the Ovaro a dozen feet closer to his target and sent the lariat spinning through the air. She suddenly sensed danger and looked up just in time to see the loop coming down to fall over her. Fargo pulled and the lasso tightened around her. She gave a small shriek as she came out of the saddle, and the cry turned to an oath as she landed on her rear in a clump of brush.

Fargo rode up quickly, pulling her to her feet with the lariat. Arms pinned to her sides, she spit fury at him as he dismounted. "You bastard," she said. "You gave me your word."

"Try again. All I said was that you didn't give me much choice at the point of a gun," Fargo said. "Now you're going to talk, honey." He scooped up the Henry which had fallen to the ground before he loosened the coil of the lasso around her. "You've a name. Start with that," he growled.

"Sally Jamison," she muttered, and rubbed her rear with one hand. "You didn't have to be so damn rough."

"Same to you, honey," Fargo said. "How come you know so much about me?"

"General Taylor's been talking a lot about your coming."

"That doesn't explain everything you said."

"Tim Greenspun," she said. "My folks were good friends with him. He used to talk about you often." Fargo's eyes stayed on her as he considered her reply. He'd broken many a trail for Tim Greenspun, and Tim had come to know him better than most. He decided to accept the answer, as far as it went.

"Let's have the rest of it," he said. "Why do you have to be part of General Taylor's wagon train?"

"That's my business for now."

"Damn, you've more brass than a bar rail."

"I'll tell you when the time comes for it," she said, and Fargo stared at her. Without the big Henry she was hardly formidable, a small girl with a neat figure that matched the pleasant prettiness of her face. But her light-brown eyes still blazed determination and he shook his head at her.

"There won't be any time, Sally Jamison," he said. "Get on your horse and ride."

"You saying you won't help me?" she flung at him, and he heard the incredulousness in his own voice.

"Help you? You're lucky I don't turn you over my knee and fan your tail!" He emptied the shells from the rifle and tossed it at her. She caught it deftly with one hand and, with something close to a flounce, spun and pulled herself into the saddle. She paused to glare back at him, her light-brown eyes blazing

"You'll take that wagon train out and I'll be part of it," she said. "Or you'll be sorry, Skye Fargo."

"*Git!*" he barked and she dug her heels into the brown mare and sent the horse galloping downhill. He watched her go till she was out of sight in the foliage before he returned to the saddle. He turned and rode back down the other side of the hill to the road. The incident had been as strange as it was unexpected. Maybe she was just a wild, headstrong hellion all caught up in her own wild concerns. Maybe he'd seen the last of her, he told himself, and grimaced, for he knew it was a hollow wish. She was too full of fire to just back off from whatever it was that drove her. But maybe he could meet with General Morton Taylor and get the wagon train rolling without delay. The man had contacted him by letter and enclosed the kind of up-front money only a fool could ignore. Of course, he had some questions to ask the general before he took the job, Fargo reflected. But he couldn't think of answers that would make him turn down the kind of money offered.

He reached the road and put the Ovaro into a trot. Claysville was still a good distance away, west of Spanish Peak in Colorado territory, and he was grateful for the road that cut through the heavy forest on both sides. He'd gone perhaps another mile when the road took a slow incline upward, and he reached the top to see the road stretching out in an almost straight line. He also saw the lone rider coming toward him, and his hand went to the Colt at his side. The rider came closer and he took in long black hair; thick and free-flowing black eyes; an aquiline nose; a full, wide mouth; and everything held together by smoothly sensuous olive skin. She wore a yellow shirt and black riding britches and he saw somewhat long breasts that swayed beautifully in unison as she rode. Her beauty seemed a product of two cultures, one north of the border, the other south.

The young woman came to a halt and surveyed him with a cool appraisal that bordered on arrogance but didn't quite mask the appreciation in it. "Skye Fargo, the Trailsman," she said and her voice was low, almost husky.

"Not again," Fargo bit out.

"I beg your pardon," she frowned.

"Nothing. Go on," Fargo said.

"You are the Trailsman, right?" the young woman said and he nodded.

"How'd you know?" he asked.

"I was told you rode a really magnificent Ovaro," she said. "And you're expected today."

He let his eyes take in the slow swell of the longish breasts that formed fully rounded cups at the bottoms. "I hope you're the real welcoming committee," he remarked.

"I wouldn't exactly say that," she answered coolly.

"What would you exactly say?" Fargo pushed at her.

"No wagon train," she snapped.

"Want to run that past again?" Fargo frowned.

"You're not going to break trail for that wagon train," she said. "It's not going out."

Fargo's lips pursed as he studied her. "Same melody, different words," he grunted.

"What's that mean?" she frowned.

"Never mind. Tell me more," Fargo said.

"I'll double what General Taylor has offered you. All you have to do is take it and leave," she said.

"That'd be a powerful lot of money," Fargo said.

"I know that, but that wagon train must not go out," she replied. "Without you, it won't."

"He could find somebody else," Fargo suggested.

"Not like you and he needs the very best," she answered. "And it'd take a long time to find someone else." She met his curious stare with an upward tilt of her chin. "I've the money with me. You can just take it and go back."

"If I say no, honey, what then?" Fargo asked.

"You're a dead man," Skye Fargo. One way or the other, you are not taking out that wagon train," she answered.

"Why not? What's all this to you, honey?" Fargo questioned.

"That is none of your concern," the beautiful young woman said.

Fargo probed into the coolly lovely face that wore both pleasant sensuousness and aristocratic hauteur. She was as different from Sally Jamison as her demands were. "I want some reasons," he said. "You could give me your name, too."

"No reasons. No name. Just take the money and leave," she said. "You can leave alive and richer, or dead and poorer."

"You've a way of putting things, don't you?" Fargo smiled and she shrugged and her breasts pressed into the yellow shirt for an instant. "Just how do you figure I'll be dead?"

"There are three guns trained on you this very moment," she said. Fargo kept his face impassive and his eyes on her. "I wouldn't like to see that happen. You're still young and good-looking and I'm sure there are lots of ladies still waiting for you."

"I sure hope so."

"Then you'll take the money and leave?"

He kept his eyes steady on her, refused to give her the satisfaction of looking past her into the trees that lined the road. But his thoughts raced and something told him she wasn't making hollow threats. She didn't seem the kind for that, and the thick woods could hide a lot more than three men. He turned words in his mind. If she had three gunmen trained on him, he wanted them out in the open. "You know what I think?" He smiled. "I think you're full of shit."

He watched her black eyes grow blacker. "You're making a mistake, Fargo," she warned icily.

"And you're as dumb as you are beautiful if you think I'm going to just believe you," he slid at her, and saw her frown as she considered his reply.

"Yes, perhaps that is asking too much of someone such as you," she said. She raised her left arm into the air and brought it down again slowly, and Fargo looked past her to where the three riders carefully pushed out of the trees. He sized up the three men immediately as they halted, kept distance between themselves. Two held rifles, raised and aimed, and the third held a five-shot, single-action Joslyn army revolver. All three were pick-up gun hands, none carrying a real gunfighter's weapons and each too tense. But there were three and they had their firepieces aimed. He needed a few seconds, just enough to make them hesitate. "Satisfied?" the young woman asked with an edge of cold triumph.

Fargo shrugged. "Guess so," he said. "I never was one for getting myself shot. You say you've the money with you?"

"Yes, right here," the young woman said and drew an envelope from her skirt pocket.

"Guess you made yourself a deal," Fargo said and moved the Ovaro toward her horse, a dark-gray gelding with black spots on its rump.

She allowed a tiny smile to curl the edges of her wide but attractive mouth. "I'm glad you're not as difficult as I'd heard you were," she said as he halted alongside her. He started to reach out for the envelope when suddenly the casual movement changed into a lightninglike lunge. He closed one hand around her forearm and yanked and she flew from her horse into his arms. He let himself go backward from the Ovaro with her and heard her curse of surprise and anger. He cast a quick glimpse at the three gunmen and saw they looked on with the moment of hesitation he wanted, unable to get a clear shot and uncertain whether to risk firing at all.

Fargo rolled when he hit the ground with the girl and only pushed her aside when he reached the heavy brush at the edge of the road. He yanked at his Colt while she half fell, half ran through the brush and he then took quick aim at the man with the Joslyn army pistol. He fired and the man flew backward from the saddle as though he'd been hit by a huge, invisible baseball bat. "Shoot, damn you, shoot," he heard the young woman scream and the two remaining riders dived from their horses as Fargo fired again. He saw his first shot graze the shirt collar of one of the men as he dived to the ground, and Fargo drew deeper into the brush, held back another shot as the two figures disappeared into the trees. "Get him. Go after him," the girl ordered from the edge of the treeline and Fargo half rose, shook the low branch of a tree, and dived onto his stomach as four shots whistled over his head to slam into tree trunks.

He stayed on his stomach, reloaded the Colt, and kept his head down as he let his ears become his eyes. The two men were making their way through the brush toward him, and he followed their paths by the rustle of leaves and the sound of branches being pressed back. One moved away from the other, he detected, a second path of sound opening to his right. They were attempting an encircling movement, aware that their quarry had to be somewhere in the brush in front of them. Fargo carefully let his long legs stretch out and position himself. Once he fired, he'd reveal his position and one or the other would immediately send a fusillade of hot lead his way. Fargo grimaced and raised his hand with the big Colt in it. He knew what he'd have to do to strike and stay alive after it.

He peered through the leaves and the brush and saw the man come into view, crawling carefully, the rifle held in front of him and ready to fire. He listened again, let his wild-creature hearing pick out sounds. The second one was not more than a few yards to the right of the first. Fargo let the man come closer, waited until the searcher halted. The man had a narrow, tight face and as he stayed in place and swept the brush to his left with the rifle at his shoulder, Fargo waited, let him come around to the center of his circle. The sound of pulling back the hammer would seem loud as a dropped stone in the silence; Fargo's thumb rested on the hammer and he waited another ten seconds. He pulled the hammer back and fired almost in one motion, and the bullet grazed the side of the rifle barrel and smashed into the man's face. Fargo flung himself sideways instantly as the shower of red spray exploded to coat the leaves. He heard the explosion of bullets that thudded into the ground where he'd lain, and he rolled again as two more bullets plowed into the soil closer to him.

Landing against the base of a tree trunk, he stayed flat, skidded himself in a half circle, and spotted the brush move to his right. The third man still hunted for him, and he caught a glimpse of a hat that vanished behind a clump of tall brush. Another sound suddenly interrupted, the sharp tattoo of hoofbeats racing away. The girl had decided to take her horse and bolt. Fargo grunted and he saw the brush suddenly quiver. The third man had made the same decision, and Fargo rose, drove powerful legs through the brush toward the road, and reached the edge of the trees in time to see the man vault onto his horse.

"Hold it right there, mister," Fargo shouted. The man half spun in the saddle, fired a wild shot from the rifle, dug his heels into the horse's side, and began to race away. Fargo took a moment to aim. He wanted the man alive and able to answer questions. He fired and saw the man fall forward, drop the rifle and twist his body in pain as the bullet slammed into his shoulder. But he managed to cling to the horse's mane and prevent himself from falling. Fargo cursed as he ran to where the Ovaro waited. He leaped onto the horse and bent low in the saddle as he sent the pinto into a gallop. The fleeing assailant stayed on the road. Fargo closed quickly, seeing the man glance back in pain and fright as he tried desperately to coax more speed from his horse. But Fargo drew almost abreast of him in minutes and the man surprised him by suddenly reining up. His horse reared as he was yanked to a halt. Fargo skidded past before he could bring the pinto to a halt, and he saw the man had slid from the horse's rump to the ground and had started into the trees on foot.

"Come back here, you damn fool," Fargo shouted, and leaped to the ground, the Colt in his hand. He heard the man crashing through the woods and ran after him, quickly spotting his quarry as the man half stumbled, half ran, one arm hanging loosely. Fargo closed in on the fleeing figure. He dropped down when the man suddenly whirled and fired three wild shots from a sixgun in his right hand. Fargo rose as the man turned and started to run again, and he raised the Colt, aimed, and fired again. The man's gasp of pain came loud and clear as he fell, and Fargo ran forward, reached the figure as the man pulled himself to his feet again, swayed, and fell to the ground. The second shot had gone clean through his other shoulder, Fargo saw as he reached down and yanked the man up against the base of a tree. He kicked the man's gun away from where it had fallen from his fingers.

"I need a doc. I'm bleeding to death," the man groaned.

"Talk first," Fargo rasped. "Who was she?"

"I don't know. She never gave us her name," the man said.

"If you're lying you'll need the undertaker, not a doctor," Fargo said.

"Not lyin'," the man said. "She hired us three days ago."

"And you don't know anything more about her," Fargo pressed.

"Nothin'," the man said. "Christ, I hurt bad. Get me to a doc."

"Claysville's a long ride," Fargo said.

"In my saddlebag . . . bandages," the man gasped, and Fargo holstered the Colt and strode to the horse. He had lifted the flap of the saddlebag when he caught the faint sound, a rush of breath from sudden painful exertion. He dropped before he whirled, and the shot grazed his head and slammed into the saddlehorn. The horse bolted, but Fargo had the Colt out of its holster in a split-second motion and fired at the figure against the tree. The shot slammed into the man's abdomen and he seemed to erupt in a shower of entrails. The gun in his hand fell to the ground and Fargo saw the opened buttons of the shirt where he'd had the second gun hidden inside.

"Goddamn fool," Fargo muttered, and rose to his

feet. If the man had known more, he'd not be telling it now. Fargo grunted silently and walked to the Ovaro. He climbed onto the horse and slowly rode away and felt the frown that dug into his brow. A nice, peaceful day had suddenly become not at all peaceful. A nice, simple job of breaking trail for a wagon train had suddenly become not at all simple. Two lovely young women had threatened to kill him, one if he didn't take the wagon train out, the other if he did. It was less than a promising beginning. Fargo half smiled. But it promised not to be dull, either.

ROUGH RIDERS

☐ **THEY CAME TO CORDURA by Glendon Swarthout.** The classic Western by the author of *The Shootist.* Major Thorn was supposed to be a coward, the five men under him were supposed to be heroes, and the woman they guarded was supposed to be a wench. But as the outlaw army closed in on them in the heat of the desert, the odds could change—and so could the people. "Excitement from start to finish."—*The New York Times* (146581—$2.75)*

☐ **SKINNER by F.M. Parker.** John Skinner never really liked to kill—until now ... against a thieving, murdering gang that held the woman he loved for ransom. Wild and tough as the mustangs he bred in the harshest badlands in the West, Skinner yearned to have the ruthless gang in his sights. Pulling the trigger was going to be a pleasure....
(138139—$2.75)

☐ **THE HIGHBINDERS by F.M. Parker.** They left him for dead ... and now it was his turn to kill. A vicious gang of outlaws were out for miner's gold and young Tom Galletin stood alone against the killing crew ... until he found an ally named Pak Ho. Together they had to cut down all the odds against them ... with Galletin's flaming Colt .45 and Pak Ho's razor-sharp, double edged sword. (149424—$2.75)

☐ **THE RAWHIDERS by Ray Hogan.** Forced outside the law, Matt Buckman had to shoot his way back in. Rescued from the savage Kiowas by four men who appeared suddenly to save him, Matt Buckman felt responsible for the death of one and vowed to ride in his place. Soon he discovered that filling the dead man's boots would not be easy ... he was riding with a crew of killers ... killers he owed his life to....(143922—$2.75)

☐ **COLTER by Quint Wade.** Colter's brother was gunned down in a hellhole Arizona town, and nothing was going to stop Colter from finding his killer ... not the hired guns who left him for dead, not the sheriff who told him to clear out, not even the cold-as-steel cattle baron who owned everyone in town. But lots of men were going to stop his bullets as he blazed a trail to the truth.... (151925—$2.75)

*Prices slightly higher in Canada.
